BENEVOLENT

Erin A. Jensen

2018 Benevolent
Text copyright © 2018 Erin A. Jensen
All Rights Reserved
Dream Waters Publishing LLC
ISBN: 0-9971712-9-4
ISBN 13: 978-0-9971712-9-7

To every reader out there who is struggling just to make it through the day; you are beautiful and you were put on this earth for a reason. Don't dim your light because others are too blind to see that.

To Chris for supporting this venture and believing in me from the beginning.

And to Misha Collins for inspiring this story with your portrayal of Castiel and your benevolent heart.

PREFACE

I don't normally do this. None of my other books include a preface, but *Benevolent* isn't like my other books. This story took shape in my mind of its own accord and refused to wait its turn to be written. (Hopefully the readers who've been waiting for the next book in my Dream Waters series will find it in their hearts to forgive me.) When I first began writing stories, one of my main goals was to use my gift to help make this world a better place in some way; and that's what I hope to accomplish with *Benevolent*. I knew almost from the get-go of this project that I would be donating one-hundred percent of the proceeds from this book to Random Acts. Because this story holds such a special place in my heart, I'd like to share a bit about how it came to be before diving into the narrative.

While writing the fourth book in my urban fantasy series, I was spending my downtime watching *Supernatural* on Netflix with my son and husband. After watching an episode of the show one evening, I sat down to write; but for some inexplicable reason I couldn't get the show's utterly endearing trench-coat-wearing angel out of my head. As easily distracted and prone to procrastination as the next writer, I decided

Castiel might be the inspiration for a future story; and I abandoned my work in progress to surf the internet and find out if Castiel was the name of an actual angel in the Bible. In a roundabout way, that search led me to The Book of Enoch. Intrigued by the story of the Watchers, I started reading about the lost books of the Bible, thinking maybe my next writing project would stem from the story of those fallen angels.

Still determined to turn distraction into inspiration, I watched some clips of Castiel's scenes in *Supernatural* on YouTube. One clip led to another, and the clips of Castiel led me to clips of Misha Collin's appearances at *Supernatural* conventions, until I stumbled upon one that really spoke to me. While telling the story of a young girl at a past convention, who confided that *Supernatural* was the only thing that'd kept her going during a difficult time, the actor was moved to tears. This resonated deeply with me because television was my means of escape during a painful portion of my young life. Immersing your mind in the fictional world of strong, fiercely protective, kind-hearted characters makes it easy to fantasize about living in their world under their protection. Not only do Misha Collins and his co-stars understand that, but they also embrace it. The SPNFamily Crisis Support Network—formed by Random Acts (the charitable organization Misha co-founded) in partnership with IMAlive, TWLOHA and

Pop Culture Hero Coalition—is proof of just how committed these actors are to helping their fans in times of need.

Moved by what I'd learned about the actor who plays my favorite angel, but still searching for that Castiel-inspired spark that would fuel my next story (aka procrastinating online), I eventually found myself on Misha Collin's Twitter feed. As I scrolled through an endless string of comments on one of his tweets, I discovered that most of the commenters' profile pictures were either pictures of Misha, or pictures of themselves with him. One picture in particular caught my eye. It was a picture of a girl in her teens, standing beside Misha with his arm around her shoulders, and the look on her face spoke volumes to me. She was smiling, but there was so much sorrow in her eyes. It was obvious that this moment meant the world to her. Then I looked at Misha's expression. His kind eyes and benevolent smile suggested that he knew exactly how much that moment meant to her; and for that split second, he was every bit the angel she needed him to be. The picture moved me to tears and became the inspiration for this story.

Soon after I started writing this book, I read about an upcoming *Supernatural* convention in Cleveland that was part of the Giving Back Tour. Misha Collins was going to be headlining the event; and Random

Acts representatives would be overseeing the convention's Charitable Quest to raise money for Family Promise of Greater Cleveland, a local non-profit agency that aids homeless families. The Cleveland convention was also going to include a Creative Quest, a competition where fans could submit an original creative work with a *Supernatural*/rock-and-roll theme to be displayed and judged during the convention. The spirit of Cleveland's charity-centric convention was so in line with the theme of my story and my goal for the book that it almost felt like a sign. I decided to go to the convention, enter *Benevolent* in the Creative Quest, and speak to the Random Acts representatives on site about setting my book up as a fundraiser. To incorporate the competition's rock-and-roll theme into my story, I reworked the chapters I had already written to include a playlist that Abigail's best friend made for her before he passed away. Each chapter title is a song from the playlist, and I listened to that song on repeat while I wrote the chapter.

The Cleveland convention turned out to be an incredible experience. *Benevolent* was the winning entry in the prose category of the Creative Quest. The Random Acts representatives at the convention were a tremendous help with setting this book up as a fundraiser. Most importantly, the convention allowed me to experience firsthand what it truly means to be a part of the *Supernatural* family. It was moving to witness such a unique and diverse group of individuals all coming together to celebrate this show with the miraculous ability to turn strangers into family.

The fans I met at the convention and online cheered me on as I worked toward getting this book published, they provided feedback on cover designs, and they welcomed me into their family with open arms. I cannot thank each and every one of you enough for all your support and encouragement. The profits from this book will go to Random Acts, but the story itself is for my *Supernatural* family. You all are amazing, and your words and actions have inspired me in so many ways. I hope you never stop being your uniquely beautiful selves!

If you'd like to read my story the same way I wrote it—with the songs playing as background music—you can find a link to Abigail's playlist on my website:

erinajensen.com

Angel of God,

my guardian dear,

to whom his love commits me here;

ever this day be at my side,

to light and guard,

to rule and guide.

—Baltimore Manual of Prayers (1888)

1

"Dust in the Wind"

Kansas

They say your life flashes before your eyes when you're dying, but for me, it wasn't just a quick flash. As I lay in that cold sterile hospital bed—enduring the slow progression of cancer's inevitable victory over my body—the highlight reel of my life played out at an unhurried pace, allowing me to relive each moment over again.

Why did my final montage play out differently than most? I couldn't say for sure. Maybe a slow death allowed more time for reflection, or maybe my vivid imagination just refused to conform to the normal way of doing things. That wasn't for me to know. I was just grateful for the distraction from my pain.

As my mind drifted back to the past, I shut my eyes and gave myself over to it because this would be my last chance to see his face before I left this world...

...Mousy soft-spoken little creature that I was, I wasn't a particularly popular child. In fact, I didn't make my first true friend until the third grade. Danny Cobb was the kindest soul I had ever met. Fortunately for me, he was also the most clueless when it came to interacting with his fellow grade-schoolers. Social awkwardness was the common ground from which the seed of our friendship took root—fiercely and protectively—empowering us to weather the cruel storm of our formative years.

My cancer-riddled brain was a bit fuzzy on the details of exactly how our friendship had begun eighty-something years earlier. What had stuck with me through all those years were the moments that truly mattered: the day in fifth grade when Danny stood up to the bully who tormented me during recess and walked away with a black eye and a busted lip...the day in eighth grade when he confided that he was attracted to boys but he was too afraid of his Catholic parents' reaction to tell them...the day we skipped school and snuck back to his house to watch the all-day *Supernatural* marathon and drool over our television heart-throbs...the day in ninth grade when he collapsed during math class and they wheeled him out of school on a stretcher...the day my mother told me that Danny wasn't going to get better because the cancer was too far gone…and the day I said goodbye to my dear friend…

…I was curled up under a blanket on the living room couch, attempting to drown my sorrows in a fictional world where angels and demons roamed the earth and beautifully flawed heroes battled monsters to protect the unsuspecting masses from harm. As much as I usually enjoyed mooning over my favorite trench-coat-wearing angel, I could only stare absently at the screen. My heart just wasn't in it that night because Danny's mother had called my house a few hours earlier to inform my mom that the doctors didn't expect my friend to live through the night. When my mom broke the news to me, I begged her to take me to the hospital so I could say goodbye, but she insisted it wouldn't be right to intrude because Danny's mother didn't want me to see him like that. Mrs. Cobb felt that it would be better for me to remember my best friend the way he was before the cancer ate away at his body. But who cared what *she* felt? It was Danny's life that was slipping away. His feelings were the only feelings that ought to matter, and I knew in my heart that he would want me to be there.

Adrift in a sea of grief, I sat and stared at the credits as they scrolled down the screen at the end of the episode. The fact that the show was over didn't even register until an obnoxiously loud car insurance commercial snapped me out of it enough to hunt for the remote and turn off the television. I stood up from the couch with a weary sigh. Then I headed down the hall at a snail's pace, locked myself in the bathroom and went through the motions of getting ready for bed on autopilot. All the while, I prayed that my mom would change her mind and offer to take me to the hospital so I could say goodbye to Danny.

When I finished getting ready for bed, I headed straight to my room without bothering to say goodnight to the woman who refused to take me where I desperately needed to go. I shut my bedroom door a little louder than I needed to, slipped into my comfiest pajamas and grabbed my smartphone and earbuds off the top of my dresser. As I turned around, my eyes settled on the top drawer of my desk across the room and my heart sank inside my chest.

A few weeks after Danny had learned that his cancer was incurable, he gave me a letter in a sealed envelope and sent me a link to a playlist that he'd put together for me. He made me promise not to check either of them out until *after he was gone.* I had kept my word. The envelope still sat unopened in the top drawer of my desk, and I'd resisted the overwhelming urge to click on the link to the playlist. Every time I considered taking a peek at it, a sinking feeling had settled in the pit of my stomach. *Don't play it until after*

I'm gone, Abbie. It almost felt like opening the envelope or clicking on the link would somehow be sealing his fate and sentencing him to death, *but now...* What harm could looking at the letter do? My friend was already on death's doorstep. After everything the two of us had been through together, I couldn't believe it was all going to end without me ever getting the chance to say goodbye to him. The least I could do was read the goodbye that Danny had written to me, and hope to God that he knew I'd be there in a heartbeat if I had any say in the matter.

That painfully familiar sinking feeling settled in the pit of my stomach as I walked to my desk and pulled the drawer open. I reached in with a trembling hand, took the envelope out and clutched it to my chest as I dropped into an armchair beside the window. Then I drew my legs up onto the seat, and hugged them close to my body as I took a few deep breaths to calm my nerves; but my hands just wouldn't stop shaking. So, I propped the envelope up on my knees with a resolute sigh. *I'm so sorry I can't be there to say goodbye to you, Danny.*

Childish as it sounds, I mouthed a silent prayer that somehow Danny would get my mental message and know how much I wanted to be there for him. *This was all just so freaking unfair.* Danny had always been there for me when I needed him. I wanted to slap both our mothers for being too stupid and selfish to let me be there for him when he needed me the most. Keeping us apart wasn't better for me or Danny, it was easier for *them* because they wouldn't have to witness our tearful goodbye.

My unsteady hands fumbled with the seal on the envelope for a moment before it gave way. As I slipped the letter out, a stray tear slid down my cheek and dripped from my chin, but I was careful to keep the pages out of its path. A torrent of nausea rose up from deep inside me, crashing over me in a violent wave as I smoothed the precious sheets of paper out. I squeezed my eyes shut and focused on breathing in and out until the queasiness subsided. Then I opened my eyes and read Danny's parting words to me.

Abbie,

I know you so well that it almost feels like the two of us are halves of the same whole. I can picture exactly what you look like while you're reading this. You're curled up on a comfy piece of furniture, hugging your legs to your chest with tears streaming down your cheeks. I wish to God that I could be there to dry those tears. If it's any consolation, I'm bawling like a baby as I write this letter to you. But you probably knew that already.

I want you to know that my life has been so much richer because of you. You filled the second half of my life with more joy than I would've guessed it was possible to squeeze into seven short years. My heart is bursting with love for you as I write this, almost as if all the love I meant to share with you over the next eighty years is pouring out onto this page.

It's funny. As much as I've always loved to write, I'm finding it almost impossible to express everything that I want to say to you. I've been trying to finish this letter for days now and I can't, because I don't want to say goodbye to you *ever*. I want to stay right here and share decades full of laughter and tears with you, Abbie. I want us to watch each other get married (even though I know you'll never find a husband as awesome as me, and if fate had given me the chance, I doubt I could've found a husband as dear as you). I want us to celebrate all the milestones—birthdays, holidays, the turning of the seasons—side by side, and I want the two of us to grow old together. I just can't bring myself to say goodbye to you, so I'm not going to.

I've always felt that nothing stirs up more emotion than a song that speaks to the heart and expresses exactly what you're feeling when you listen to it. If a song is playing—during a special moment in your life—every time you hear that song, it will bring you right back to that moment and all the emotions you felt when you first heard it will come flooding back to you. So, that's what I've decided to give you, songs that speak to the heart, to make you feel like a part of me is still there with you. Whenever you need me, you can listen to a song from your playlist and know that I'm out there somewhere, listening to the same song and waiting for the day when I can pull you into a bear hug and tell you how much I've missed you.

Because I want to put a smile on your face, and hopefully even make you laugh after you've worked through the grief, I decided to load the playlist up with a bunch of rock-and-roll songs. Yeah, I know. You're a diehard indie music girl, but these songs are supposed to remind you of me. So there. I get the final say in our epic debate because I know you'll give my type of music the chance you refused to give it when I was around, since these songs are my way of remaining a part of your life. Play them when you miss me, curse me a little for including so many rock songs; then admit that I was right all along after you fall in love with them. Wherever I am, just know that I'll be smiling down at you with a big *I told you so.*

In all seriousness, this playlist isn't something I slapped together quickly. I've spent the past few weeks choosing the perfect songs, songs that are sure to win you over once you give them a chance. In honor of my favorite *Supernatural* character, some of the songs are straight up Dean Winchester-approved classic rock songs. In fact, a couple songs on the list are sure to put a smile on your face because you'll associate them with *Supernatural* episodes. But I didn't torture you too much. Almost every subgenre of rock is represented on the list: progressive rock, folk rock, alternative rock, grunge rock, hard rock, psychedelic rock, indie rock, blues rock, roots rock, soft rock, pop rock. (Yeah, I did my homework.)

So, let me explain why I picked the songs that made it onto this list. I know you, Abbie. I know most of your favorite songs are on the slower side. I know you love a singer with a voice that you can identify after just a couple verses; and I know that a gorgeous harmony trumps pretty much everything else in your book. Even though you've always insisted I'm tone-deaf and I only love rock music because I can sing along just by screaming the lyrics, I know a perfect harmony when I find one. Our friendship is the ultimate perfect harmony, and I've treasured it since the day it started.

Okay, now on to the playlist. I added a couple Sting songs because Sting's voice is about as unique as a fingerprint, and the songs of his that I picked are on the slower side. I included "Your Song" because it's also on the slow side and guaranteed to move you, but I went with the angelic-sounding Ellie Goulding version instead of the classic Elton John because I knew you'd love her voice. "Nights In White Satin" by The Moody Blues is a beautiful song with a dreamy tempo that's sure to win you over. Kansas's "Carry on

Wayward Son" needs no explaining to a *Supernatural* fangirl like you, and "Dust in the Wind" will be one of your favorites for sure. It's got a slow tempo, beautiful harmony and lyrics that'll bring tears to your eyes. I threw in a Creedence Clearwater Revival song because I'm pretty sure at least one of their songs was in an episode of *Supernatural*, and I just love their music. The Beatles' "Hey Jude" is on the list because they're the freaking Beatles. You're the tone-deaf one if you can't appreciate their songs. Since it would be criminal to exclude the king from a rock-and-roll playlist, Elvis Presley's "Can't Help Falling in Love" made the final cut. The king's velvet voice and the lyrics to this song are sure to melt your heart. Simon and Garfunkel's "Bridge Over Troubled Waters" made the list because they're the masters of harmony, and although they're more folk-rock-ish, they're in the Rock-and-Roll Hall of Fame (told you I did my homework). There are a bunch more songs. Some of them are by indie bands and some aren't even rock music, just songs I knew you'd love. I know you hate country music, but I still included one Willie Nelson song. I figured you wouldn't be too mad at me for adding it because the song I chose is "Blue Eyes Crying In the Rain." Deny that you like the song all you want, but it was playing at the end of the *Supernatural* episode where Castiel said goodbye to Claire Novak and I saw the tears in your eyes as your favorite angel watched her taxi drive away. Okay, I'm not going to ramble on forever and list every song that made the final cut, but you're eventually going to fall in love with every song on the list. I'd bet my life on it. (Okay...sorry. Bad joke.)

Play these songs when you miss me, Abbie. Choose one that matches your mood, close your eyes and imagine me sitting there listening along with you. Until we meet again, please know that I love you more than anyone or anything, and I always will.

All my love,

Danny

I choked back a sob as I unlocked my phone and brought up the link to Danny's playlist. Then I plugged my earbuds into the phone, stuck them in my ears and started the music. "Dust in the Wind" by Kansas was the first song on the list. I was only a few verses in when the tears started streaming down my cheeks. My heart physically ached as I listened to the lyrics that so perfectly fit the moment, but I didn't have the heart to stop the song because Danny had chosen each one with such care. I waited it out with my heart throbbing in my chest and stopped the music the instant the first song ended, vowing to listen to all of them when I was a bit more prepared to handle it.

I tugged my earbuds out of my ears, closed the playlist and glanced at the time on my phone. It was forty-three minutes past midnight, way past my mom's bedtime. It was pretty safe to assume that she wasn't going to have a change of heart at this point. *Chalk that up as one more unanswered prayer to add to my list.* Praying seemed about as useful as tossing a coin in a wishing well or wishing on a falling star. I wasn't sure why the hell I still bothered.

I stood up from the chair, squeezed my eyes shut and held the letter close to my heart while I whispered a teary goodbye to my friend. Then I opened my eyes and blinked back the tears as I sat my phone down on my desktop next to Danny's letter.

I shuffled across the room with a heavy heart, crawled into bed and cried myself to sleep, aching in the knowledge that I'd most likely wake in a world that my friend no longer inhabited.

That was the first night that he ever came to me in a dream.

"Would you like to say your goodbyes now, Abigail?" a male voice inquired from the foot of my bed.

A deep male voice—rousing me from sleep in the middle of the night—probably should've terrified me, but it didn't because this man's voice was a familiar comfort.

I sat up and rubbed the sleep from my eyes, which was pointless since I was obviously still dreaming. There at the foot of my bed, stood my favorite television angel, dressed in a button-down shirt, crooked necktie, and that iconic trench coat of his. He was beautiful, flawless bone structure, stylishly mussed-up hair, and piercing blue eyes that looked far too wise to belong to this man at the peak of physical perfection.

I blinked my eyes a few times to reboot my senses, but he still stood there waiting for an answer. "Castiel?" I muttered in a groggy whisper, "Am I dreaming?"

He smiled at me with more compassion than I'd ever witnessed in any human set of eyes. "Yes. You are, but that doesn't make this any less real."

"I've lost my mind," I muttered as my eyes filled with tears. "My best friend is dying and I'm sitting on my bed, talking to a fictional angel."

His brilliant blue eyes brimmed with sorrow as he shook his head. "You are talking to a real angel. I chose this form because the fictional angel is a comfort to you."

I blinked my eyes a few more times, expecting him to be gone each time my eyelids lifted. "What?"

His apologetic frown did nothing to detract from his beauty. "There isn't much time to explain, Abigail. Danny is not long for this world, and I know how much he means to you. His mother is wrong to deny you the opportunity to say goodbye."

"How would we get there?" I muttered, ignoring the way my heart ached at the angel's words. If I focused on that pain, I would fall apart, this dream would morph into something nightmarish, and I'd lose this imaginary chance to see my friend one last time. "I'm pretty sure I'm not allowed to leave the house with strange men who slip into my bedroom in the middle of the night."

"I'm not a man," he whispered as he touched a hand to my foot.

The instant he touched me, my room melted away and I found myself sitting on Danny's hospital bed.

My eyes filled with tears at the sight of all the tubes and wires connected to my friend's brittle body. I looked up and felt comforted by the angel's presence.

"He can hear you," the angel standing beside the bed whispered.

"Danny," I croaked as I slid closer to him, "it's me, Abigail."

"Abbie…" It seemed to take a tremendous effort for Danny to lift his eyelids, but a smile spread across his ashen face as he looked up at me. "I was afraid I wouldn't get to say goodbye."

"I'll tell her goodbye for you, Danny." Until his mother spoke, I didn't realize she was seated in the corner of the room. My heart hammered in my chest as I turned toward the woman who'd refused to let me say goodbye to my friend, but a pang of sorrow gripped me the instant I laid eyes on her. I couldn't possibly be mad at this puffy-eyed woman who sat there, hunched in on herself, hugging her sides as she gripped a crumpled tissue for dear life. Grief loomed over the poor woman like a specter, poised and ready to swallow her the instant her child drew his last breath.

"She's here now," Danny muttered in a voice much too frail for a fifteen-year-old boy, "and there's a man here with her."

Tears spilled down Mrs. Cobb's cheeks as her grief-stricken eyes looked straight through me. "There's no one here but us, Danny."

"She's sitting right here on my bed." Danny's grin widened as he squinted up at the angel standing next to his bed. "Castiel. He always was your favorite…gorgeous and awkward, just like you and me."

Mrs. Cobb muffled a sob as the angel nodded a hello to Danny.

"Watch out for her," Danny whispered to the angel, "She's too precious for this ugly world."

A tear slid down my cheek as the angel took Danny's hand in his and gave it a comforting squeeze. "I have watched over her since the day she was born, Danny. She is precious, and so are you."

Danny's eyes filled with tears at the angel's words. "My church doesn't think so. According to them, I'm an abomination. Am I…going to hell…for my sins?"

Castiel gave Danny's hand another squeeze as he shook his head. "God created you just as you are, Danny. He doesn't make mistakes. You are a pure soul and it pleases Him to call you home to spend eternity in His presence. Those who consider you an abomination are the souls who are destined for hell."

Danny's bottom lip quivered as the angel let go of his hand. "Are you…here to take me?"

"No," Castiel whispered, "I am here for Abigail, but your guardian is near. You will see him when it is your time." At that, the angel turned to me. "It's time to say your goodbyes now."

I leaned forward and hugged Danny as gently as I could while holding on for dear life. "I'll always love you, Danny. No one will ever be more precious to me."

"I'm sorry I can't stay here with you, Abbie," he sobbed in a broken whisper, as I sat back and took his hand in mine, "but I'll..."

Danny's gentle brown eyes had noticeably dulled. They used to shine with such kindness and joy. The agony that darkened them now broke my heart. It was obvious that he was in an excruciating amount of pain and yet, here he was apologizing to me for leaving. I couldn't stand to see him suffer like that.

"It's alright, Danny," I whispered, forcing the words past the lump that was forming in my throat, "I know you don't want to leave...but I can see how much you're hurting...and I don't want you to suffer anymore. It's okay to let go.... I understand."

I didn't see Danny's angel, but I saw the contented smile that lit up Danny's face the instant the angel appeared. He looked so peaceful in that final moment, as he drew his last breath.

I felt something intangible break inside me at the sound of that breath, and I knew in my heart that it would haunt me for the rest of my life.

The next thing I knew, I was back in my bedroom. Tears were streaming down my cheeks, there was an unbearable ache in my chest and the fictional angel was gone...

...The voices of my loved ones were fainter now. I couldn't decipher the meaning of their words, but I recognized their voices and the rhythmic rise and fall as they joined together in prayer. I wanted so badly to tell them all how precious they were to me, but I was far beyond words.

A voice inside my head whispered, They know, Abigail. *It was my voice, but the thought had come from someone else.*

Too tired to question it, I let myself drift back to the past...

2

"Fragile"

Sting

The hours leading up to Danny's funeral were nothing but a blur. I kept my earbuds wedged in my ears and I disconnected from the world to the tune of Sting's "Fragile," the second song on Danny's playlist. I kept the song playing on repeat because the melancholy tune fit my mood to a T. Danny was right; Sting's voice was as unique as a fingerprint. It was the musical equivalent of maple sugar candy—deliciously rich and grainy, like sugary sand that melts in your mouth, or in your ears in this case—his voice was pure decadence. I focused on the heavenly voice crooning in my ears as I watched the people around me interact with absent disinterest, as if they were nothing more than two-dimensional characters in a silent movie; and I went through the motions of my day-to-day life without giving any real thought to what I was doing.

I had no memory whatsoever of getting dressed for the funeral or driving to the church, but I was pretty sure that my mom must have maneuvered me through all of it. She'd probably picked out my outfit, she may even have helped me slip into it, and she must've ushered me to the car because I couldn't remember getting in or out of it. Numb to everything that was happening around me, I was collapsing in on myself to escape the truth. This day was going to end with my friend's body buried in a box beneath six feet of dirt, and then I'd be all alone.

My first real moment of clarity since Danny's dying breath came when the organist started playing the processional hymn. I mimicked the movements of everyone around me and turned my attention toward the back of the church, and reality struck me like a knife to the chest. I felt its blade puncture my heart as I watched the men in dark suits carry Danny's coffin down the center aisle toward the front of the church.

I didn't catch a single word anyone uttered during the service. I was too busy drowning in a sea of grief, with the echo of Sting's "Fragile" still playing on repeat inside my head as I stared at the box that held my friend's body. *How was I supposed to survive in a world without Danny?* Tears spilled down my cheeks as the stoic-faced strangers around me picked up their hymnals. Their detached voices joined, voicing the heart-wrenching lyrics to the organist's hymn and twisting the knife in my chest till I physically ached from the grief.

None of these people knew Danny like I did. I wanted to jump up on my seat and scream at all of them. My friend had been a beautiful gift to all of us, and this church and its antiquated rules had made him feel like a sinner just for being himself. I wanted to shake his parents for being so stupid and blind to the truth. They should've sensed who their son really was and loved and accepted him for it before his benevolent heart stopped beating. Danny had gone to his death believing that his parents would've disowned him if he told them the truth, and *who knew?* Maybe he was right.

I hated these people. I hated Danny's clueless mother and father. I hated this emotionally constipated congregation of strangers who'd made Danny feel so uncomfortable in his own skin, and I hated my mother for being too lost in her own worries to realize how much this was killing me. As I stood there loathing all of them, the absoluteness of my new reality came crashing down on me—crushing me with relentless force, robbing the air from my lungs, and constricting my throat—until I couldn't breathe. I wasn't going to make it through this funeral. *I wasn't going to make it through life without*

Danny. I wasn't strong enough for any of this. A desperate need to flee the church gripped me as the crushing weight bearing down on me intensified, but I did my best to ignore the maddening urge to push past the people standing between me and the aisle and rush for the exit.

When the song ended, we all took our seats and I bit my lip and squeezed my eyes shut. As I prayed for the panic to subside enough for me to get through the rest of the funeral, the comforting weight of a steady hand settled on top of mine. I shifted my attention to the warmth of that hand, and solace replaced my panic as a thought that wasn't mine whispered inside my head. *You are not alone, Abigail.*

I opened my eyes and looked down at my own two hands, clasped in prayer on my lap. No one was touching me. Confused, I shut my eyes and focused on the warmth of that invisible hand. What did it matter where the sensation was coming from? Real or not, that hand was the only thing anchoring me in my seat. Without its comforting warmth, my grief would continue to swell until it swallowed me up and swept me away.

The angel came to visit my dreams again that night.

If anyone had asked me the next morning, I would've sworn that Castiel appeared at the foot of my bed *before* I fell asleep. Grief does funny things to the mind. It convinces you to see and feel and hear whatever it deems necessary to get through the pain, and you convince yourself it's all real because the truth is just too much to bear.

"You aren't alone, Abigail," his deep voice assured me from the foot of my bed.

I squeezed my eyes shut tighter and pulled the covers over my head the instant I heard his voice. I couldn't look at that angelic face. The last time those breathtakingly empathetic eyes locked with mine was the instant after Danny took his last breath. I didn't want to be reminded of that breath. The finality of that moment was going to haunt me forever. Revisiting it this soon would only twist the knife that had lodged itself in my heart during the funeral. "Please go away."

"I'm afraid I can't do that," he replied in a softer tone.

"Why not?" I muttered beneath the covers.

There was a significant pause before the angel whispered, "It's my job to watch over you."

I opened my eyes and pulled the covers off my head, half expecting to find no one there just like at the church.

But there he was, awkwardly standing at the foot of my bed as if he didn't quite know what to do.

I sat up and felt warmer the instant his eyes met mine. "Are you acting awkward like Cas to make me feel more comfortable, or do you really not know what to do?"

He cocked his head to one side as he sized me up through narrowed eyes, a gesture that perfectly mimicked his television counterpart's quizzical expression in his earliest appearances on the show. "A little of both, I suppose."

Despite my reluctance, his response actually did put me at ease. That endearing awkwardness of his felt comfortably familiar. It brought to mind the tranquility that I always experienced when I lost myself in an episode of *Supernatural*. There was something innately soothing about watching Castiel's socially clueless interactions with humans. Danny and I used to call him the patron saint of awkward souls, *our patron saint*. "So, where do we go from here?"

The angel's brow furrowed in that entirely serious Castiel-ish manner. "We don't have to go anywhere."

Despite the ache in my chest, I couldn't help smiling at his answer. "It's just an expression."

He dipped his head in a subtle nod. "Yes, I am aware of that."

"Alright," I whispered, suppressing my grin, "then what should we do now?"

The angel shook his beautiful head of perfectly mussed-up hair. "I have no idea. What would you like to do?"

"If Danny were here..." I bit my lip to blunt the ache that flared in my chest at the mention of my friend, "he would tell me a story to take my mind off my worries. He loved to make up stories."

An apologetic frown spread across the angel's face. "I don't tell stories."

"Well, then..." Too tired to give it any more thought, I yawned and dropped my head to my pillow. "Could you just sit here until I fall asleep?"

"I have no need to sit," he replied in a hushed tone, as if he were afraid to break the spell that was lulling me to sleep.

"But," my heart throbbed as the words escaped me in a broken whisper, "I have a need...to know I'm not alone."

The angel's eyes fixed on me as he nodded and stepped up to the side of my bed. Then he sat down, awkward and rigid, on the outermost edge of the mattress.

I squeezed my eyes shut to hold back the tears that were welling inside them, as I opened my mouth to tell him that he didn't have to sit next to me if it made him feel *that* uncomfortable.

But his hand settled on top of mine before I could choke out a single word, and that same comforting sensation of warmth that I'd felt at the funeral washed over me. "You are never alone, Abigail. Just try to remember that."

"Okay," I muttered as I nodded off to sleep...

...There was a lot of shuffling about in my hospital room as greetings and goodbyes were exchanged. A fresh shift of family members was taking the place of the weary. The changing of the guard—that's what my son had called it, earlier on when I was still lucid enough to take part in the conversation.

Desperate to be present in the moment with them, I concentrated on the tones of their voices and the patterns of their footfalls to determine who was coming in and who was heading out for a much-needed break.

My medication must have been wearing off because the pain had returned with a vengeance and the mental fog had lifted enough for me to comprehend the meaning of their words. I fought my way through the grogginess because I needed to see their faces.

With a great deal of effort, I managed to lift my eyelids. Their faces were a bit out of focus, but I recognized my son and daughter sitting in folding wooden chairs at my bedside.

I tried to sit up, but my weakened muscles refused to comply.

Danny noticed my struggle and leaned forward to prop a pillow under my head with the utmost care. "We're right here, Mom," he whispered as he settled back in his seat and took my hand in his.

"I love you," I replied in a thready whisper that I didn't even recognize as my own.

"We love you too," he answered in an unsteady voice.

My eyes drifted to the foot of the bed where another figure stood, casting a long shadow over the blankets that covered my legs. He was standing a bit too far from me to make out the features of his face without my glasses. "Who else is here?"

"There's no one else, Mom," Cassie sobbed as she dragged her chair right past the blurred figure to the other side of my bed to take hold of my free hand.

My eyes were still glued to the figure at the foot of my bed. "Can't you see him? He's standing right there."

"There's no one here but me and Cassie," Danny whispered as he gave my hand a reassuring squeeze.

Too tired to argue, I drifted back to the past...

3

"Bridge Over Troubled Water"
Simon and Garfunkel

My mother let me stay home from school for a week after Danny's funeral. I spent most of the week sleeping and binge-watching *Supernatural.* You would think watching our favorite show would hurt too much now that Danny was gone, but if I didn't give it too much thought I could almost convince myself that Danny was sitting on the couch watching with me. Once I slipped into that semi-trancelike state of denial, I could just sit back and lose myself in the show. For those blissful moments, I could forget that everything was wrong in my own world while I watched the Winchesters battle to put things right in their fictional world; and whenever Castiel came onscreen, that comforting warmth would spread through me just like it had at the funeral.

It was late in the evening, and I was sprawled out on the couch in the living room watching an episode of *Supernatural* and wishing Cas would make better life choices, despite the fact that I'd seen the episode already and knew he wasn't going to. *What can I say?* Worrying about the Winchesters' guardian angel was a welcome break from fretting over my own pathetic excuse for a life.

Halfway through the episode, my mother strolled into the room and scowled at the television as she shook her head. "Aren't you sick of watching this nonsense yet?"

I sat up, grabbed the remote and paused the show without saying a word because she didn't actually care whether or not I was sick of watching *Supernatural.* She just wanted to make it perfectly clear that I was a total disappointment to her, wasting my life away doing something that she considered pointless.

My mom squared her shoulders as she marched across the room and pushed the power button on the television, erasing poor Castiel from existence right in the middle of his heartfelt plea to God for guidance. "It's not good for you to spend all your time rotting your brain in front of the television, Abigail."

I knew exactly where this was going, but I kept my mouth shut and my expression neutral because my opinion was completely irrelevant to the conversation.

"I think you've had enough time to mourn," my mother announced as she plopped down on the couch next to me. "Sitting around watching silly ghost stories all day isn't healthy. It's time for you to go back to school before you get too far behind in your classes."

I bit back the words that were poised on the tip of my tongue, just begging to be spoken. What good would it do to tell her how bad things were for me at school? If she really cared, she would've noticed how miserable school made me years ago. Besides, she had her own worries to deal with. Adding to them would just be selfish, since it wouldn't actually change things for me—at least, that's what I told myself. In truth, I was just too ashamed of my situation at school to mention it to anyone.

My mother exhaled a dramatic sigh as she draped an arm across my shoulders. The gesture felt painfully awkward and forced, since she normally wasn't much for hugging or any other display of affection. "You should go get ready for bed, Abbie. Get a good night's sleep, so you won't be impossible to wake up in the morning."

I leaned into her awkward half-hug because at least she was attempting to act like she cared. It didn't seem like the appropriate time to bring up the fact that she never actually woke me up for school. More often than not, she was still in bed when I headed out the door to catch the bus in the morning.

After waiting what I imagined was the appropriate amount of time, I slipped free from her stifling almost-hug, stood up from the couch and forced a smile. "Okay, goodnight then."

Her smile seemed just as forced as she stood up beside me and whispered, "Goodnight."

With that, she headed off to the kitchen and I headed down the hall to the bathroom to get ready for bed. As I shut the bathroom door, I couldn't help wondering whether it had even occurred to her that I only said three words during that entire painful attempt at a conversation. Probably not, since that was how the majority of our conversations played out.

My mother preferred to speak *at* me rather than *to* me, which made our house dismally quiet, since it was just the two of us. My mother had chosen to run off with my father when she was quite young, and her parents had disowned her for it. Shortly after she gave birth to me, my father decided that family life just wasn't for him. He took off with some other young girl, leaving my mom to raise me on her own with no one to turn to for help but my father's parents. Grandma and Grandpa Perkins were the parents I wished I'd been born to. My visits with them were the highlights of my early childhood. After both of them died, my mom and I were on our own. Instead of showering her one remaining family member with love, my mother grew distant because she blamed me for ruining her life. Her resentful demeanor did a number on my self-esteem at an early age. That was probably more than half the reason why I'd never had the confidence to make any friends, other than Danny—and even that friendship was due to his bravery, not mine.

I did my best to ignore the ache in my stomach as I got ready for bed while my thoughts drifted to the torment that awaited me the next day. Before, even during the worst moments, I'd always been able to comfort myself with the fact that it would all melt away as soon as Danny gave me a hug and brightened my day with his latest story. Danny had been writing stories for as long as I'd known him. He had always planned on becoming a writer after he finished school, and it broke my heart that the world would never know the beauty of his words.

After I finished getting ready for bed, I went straight to my room, flipped off the lights and slid under the covers. Nauseated at the thought of facing them all without Danny, I pulled the covers up over my head.

Of course, tomorrow wouldn't be the first day that I had to brave my way through school without Danny. I'd spent plenty of days at school on my own while my friend was going through chemotherapy, but this was different. I couldn't comfort myself with the thought that school wouldn't always be this bad because now, *it would be.*

The bullies that Danny stood up to on my behalf would have no reason to stand down anymore. Of course, there was a slight possibility that they might go easy on me because my friend had just died, but I wasn't holding my breath for that to happen. My feelings had never concerned them enough to care that they filled my days with so much misery, that I dropped into bed each night, dreading the day to come and praying for the strength just to make it through. So, why would they concern themselves with my fragile emotional state now?

"Hello, Abigail," Castiel whispered from the foot of my bed.

I did my best to put on a brave face as I pulled the covers off my head and muttered, "Hello."

He stepped up to my bedside with a sorrowful smile and sat down on the edge of the mattress without waiting for me to ask him to. "Is there anything I can do?"

A tear slid down my face, and my cheeks flamed with embarrassment as I hurried to wipe it away. "You can tell me that it's my time to go now, so I don't have to go back to school tomorrow."

His infinitely compassionate eyes shimmered with tears as he frowned at my response. For such an awkward celestial being, his eyes could convey such staggering depths of emotion. "It is not your time yet, Abigail. I think you know that."

"Well…" I made a pathetic attempt at a smile and whispered, "A girl can always hope."

"Hope?" he echoed as he covered my hand with his, making me feel warm and safe, as if nothing beyond the walls of my room could ever hurt me. "Hope is for positive change that would make the world a better place."

"Maybe the world would be a better place without me in it," I muttered under my breath.

The angel's frown deepened. "I sincerely hope you don't actually believe that."

Too embarrassed to admit that I *did* believe it, I shook my head. "Why does my life have to suck so much?"

"I'm afraid I am not privy to the Lord's entire plan," he replied with an apologetic frown. "All I can tell you for certain, is that He put you on this earth for a reason. You should never doubt the light within you because others are too blind to see it."

"If there is light inside me," I muttered in a hoarse whisper, "why does everything feel so dark?"

"I truly do wish that I could reveal the reason for this dark portion of your journey, Abigail," Castiel whispered, "but it is not my place to do so. All I can do is offer to walk through the darkness with you and promise you that there will be light up ahead."

My voice was thick with unshed tears as I muttered, "I don't think I'm strong enough to do this without Danny."

The warmth that seeped from his hand seemed to pulsate for an instant as he replied, "You are much stronger than you believe yourself to be."

I dropped my eyes to his hand, resting on top of mine. "What if you're wrong?"

"I am not wrong," he replied without any hesitation. "I meant what I said to Danny at the hospital. You are precious."

I choked back the sob that erupted from my throat at the mention of Danny's final moments. "Will you stay with me until I fall asleep?"

Castiel's frown deepened for a second before he replied, "I am always with you, Abigail."

Comforted by the warmth of his presence, it didn't take me long to drift off to sleep.

As I slipped into oblivion, I almost could've sworn I heard him whisper, "I will be with you as you walk through the darkness, and I will lead you toward the light ahead if you allow me to do so. Try to remember that, Abigail."

But I probably only dreamed those whispered words because I was so desperate to hear them.

I woke the next morning, feeling surprisingly calm and well rested. Once I finished getting ready for school, I grabbed my phone, popped my earbuds in my ears and pulled up Danny's playlist. I put it on shuffle, leaving the choice of my mood music for the morning up to my phone. Stupid as it sounds, I liked to think that when I left the song choice up to chance, Danny could somehow guide the selection. I knew it was childish, but it made me feel a little less lonely and it wasn't any sillier than believing that an angel walked beside me.

Danny's musical selection for the morning was Simon and Garfunkel's "Bridge Over Troubled Water." Once again, the lyrics and the tune fit my current circumstances perfectly. I put "Bridge Over Troubled Water" on repeat and let the haunting melody drown out the world around me as I poured myself a bowl of cereal, ate my breakfast, and packed my lunch. My mom was still asleep as usual, but I was glad that I basically had the house to myself. The privacy allowed me to lose myself in Danny's music, free from the judgment in her disapproving eyes, until it was time to go out and catch the bus.

I considered missing the bus on purpose, but decided there wouldn't be any point to it. It would only piss my mom off because she'd have to drive me to school and show up late to work, and I'd still wind up in my own private hell in the end.

I left my earbuds in my ears and kept my theme music playing on repeat as I crossed the street and boarded the school bus. Dropping my eyes to the floor to avoid any unwanted eye contact, I walked down the aisle and slipped into the first empty seat. Then I tipped my head against the window and watched the world go by while Simon and Garfunkel serenaded me all the way to school.

When the bus pulled up in front of my school, I stopped the music, closed the playlist, silenced my phone and stuffed it in the front pocket of my backpack. Thankfully, I'd listened to the song enough times for the tune to get stuck in my head. So, Simon and Garfunkel's perfect harmony still echoed in my ears as I stood up and made my way off the bus.

No one walked beside me as I approached the sinister brick building and nobody took my hand as I climbed the wide set of cement steps that led up to the front doors. With absolutely no hope that anyone would ever lay himself down to bridge the troubled waters for me, I braced myself and entered the darkness.

I actually managed to make it halfway through my first day back with nothing more than the occasional whispered insult behind my back. Just as I'd suspected, none of them gave a damn that I had just lost my only friend in the world. I trudged down the path I'd been sentenced to, blindly stumbling through the darkness just like I always had. Only now, a queasy sort of ache—for the friend who had walked this path with me for so many years—gnawed at my insides. Still, I kept my head down and let the song in my head drown out the world around me as I offered up a silent prayer to make it through the rest of the school day unnoticed. Invisibility was pretty much the best I could hope for now. Unfortunately, I knew my prayers weren't going to cut it when I got to chorus. The taunting was bound to be unbearable there.

I'd wanted to drop chorus ages ago—because for some sadistic reason, the girls who sat behind me delighted in making my life a living hell—but Danny had convinced me not to quit. My kindhearted, albeit slightly tone-deaf, friend knew how much I loved to sing. So, he added chorus to his schedule and sang in a hushed off-key alto so he could sit next to me. Fortunately, the bullies didn't pick on him for singing with the girls because I was right there beside him, and the girls who sat behind me let me be for the same reason. Predators preyed on the weakest creatures—the ones who were shunned by the rest of the herd and forced to graze alone—and together, Danny and I were just enough of a herd to make the predators think twice about pouncing. But now that Danny was gone, I was a timid broken creature. I was as weak as they got.

I waited till the last second before the bell rang to walk in and take my seat in chorus, so they couldn't torment me while everyone was goofing around before class, but it made no difference. The second I sat down, two pristine pairs of expensive sneakers rammed into the back of my chair. I bit my lip and locked my muscles in place to absorb the jolt and prevent my chair from sliding across the floor, causing a mortifyingly embarrassing scene. My cheeks burned with shame, but I didn't turn around or acknowledge that I'd felt their kicks in any way. In retrospect, I suppose that might have just spurred them on. My lack of response was probably viewed as an unspoken challenge that would make it all the more satisfying when they finally broke me.

Next, came the relentless attempts to propel my chair forward—both of them pushing with their feet, combining forces to send me crashing into the row of seats ahead. I sat there, bracing my feet against the floor with all my might to anchor myself, and I pretended not to hear the snickering from the predators who were toying with me and the ever-widening circle of popular kids seated nearby who were happy to join in on the joke.

When the predatory girls got bored with pushing my seat, they started throwing bits of torn up paper in my hair. Letting the predators see any sign of weakness would be a fatal mistake on my part. So, I bit down on my tongue to quell the tears that threatened to spill from my eyes, and I retreated as far inside myself as I could while an entirely different scenario played out in my head. In my imaginary world, those predatory girls were demons and it was only a matter of time before Castiel and the Winchesters would come to my rescue and beat them back to hell where they belonged.

But the longer the paper throwing went on and the louder the muffled snickering grew, the harder it became to stay safely tucked away inside my head. I bit my lip to suppress the sob that was dangerously close to escaping my throat, and I wondered why God hated me so much. Why did these heartless girls get to be popular and loved, while I was singled out to be shunned by the herd? What had I done to deserve this on top of the death of my only friend?

"Cut it out," a male voice behind me whispered, snapping me out of my self-pitying thoughts.

I didn't turn around. No matter what, making eye contact would only provoke them.

The predatory cheerleader behind me just giggled. "What's the big deal?"

"Leave her alone." *It was Brad's voice.* Brad was a freakishly bulky thick-necked jock. His massive size and athletic prowess automatically made him an alpha in the high school predatory pack. Misfits and nerds like me and Danny instinctively gave this guy a wide berth, *so what the heck was he doing sticking up for me?*

"Oh, come on," the other alpha female behind me replied in a flirtatious whisper. "You know you'd be doing the same thing to her geeky friend if he was the one who was still alive."

How could she be so cruel? I doubted there was anything that could drive me to utter such hurtful words about another human being.

"Just stop it," Brad grunted, "and leave her alone."

The growling edge to his tone finally convinced the girls to stop, allowing me to make it through the rest of class without any more humiliation—aside from the obvious shame of being the pathetic excuse for a girl that I was.

I never asked Brad what prompted him to stick up for me that day. In fact, I never said a single word to him about anything *ever*. He was an alpha in the adolescent jungle and I was nothing but injured prey, ripe for the killing. It wasn't wise to cross those boundaries, even after he'd come to my defense.

I would never know if Brad would've stuck up for me again—or if he'd given me a one-time pass because of the death of my friend—because at the end of that hellish first day back, I went to the guidance office, dropped chorus from my schedule and picked up a study hall in its place. No one ever questioned why. I'm not sure my mom even realized I'd quit, and any teacher who cared enough to notice probably recognized me for the broken creature that I was and understood my need to cower and slink away.

To be honest, I'd never really given that moment when the alpha male mysteriously came to my aid much thought. It was just one fleeting moment in an unending string of incidents that I was desperate to bury and forget. But looking back on it in my final hours, as death breathed down my neck, I couldn't help wondering if there might have been more to it. Distanced from the emotional pain of the moment as I was now, it almost seemed like an act of divine intervention. *Could a whispered word from the spiritual plane have prompted Brad to stick up for me that day?* Perhaps I hadn't been quite as alone as I'd felt. If there was an afterlife, I made a mental note to ask about the incident after I got there.

As soon as I finished my homework the evening after that hellish first day back at school, I watched *Supernatural*—like I did every evening—to escape the loneliness of my pathetic reality. Then for the rest of the night, I retreated to the fictional world inside my head where angels and demon-hunters had my back and no one would ever dream of hurting me.

When I turned off the lights and crawled into bed at the end of that nightmarish day, I wasn't sure whether I wanted Castiel to visit my dreams. After all the years I'd spent internalizing the taunts and the name-calling, a substantial portion of it had inevitably sunken in and my sense of self-worth was irreparably damaged. Deep down, I felt like nothing more than an ugly waste of space with a blemished face, unworthy of friendship and certainly unworthy of any male's love. *How could I look that beautiful angel in the eye and talk about how pathetic I was?*

Deciding I couldn't bear for Castiel to visit, I burrowed under the covers and let the tears stream down my cheeks in the silence of my pitch-dark room.

"You're not alone, Abigail," his deep voice assured me in a hesitant whisper.

"Yes, I am," I sobbed so softly that I barely heard it myself, "I am all alone now."

I heard him step up from the foot of the bed and approach my bedside. "I know it feels that way at the moment," he whispered as the edge of the mattress dipped down, "but I promise you, you are never truly alone."

I kept the covers over my head and did my best to fight back the tears, but I couldn't stop them from falling. I had never talked about my private hell with anyone because I was too ashamed. I'd never even discussed it with Danny, *but I didn't have to say anything to him.* He'd faced the same group of tormentors, and the humiliation had been bearable because we had each other to lean on. I would have given just about anything for Danny to wrap his arms around me and tell me one of his stories that night.

I felt the angel's hand stroke my cheek through the blankets, and the tenderness of his gesture filled me with more warmth than I'd ever experienced. "You will get through this, Abigail."

This perfect ethereal creature could be off visiting the cheerleaders' dreams. *So, why was he wasting his time with a loser like me?*

"You are not a loser," he whispered, even though I was sure I hadn't said that out loud. "You were created by God and He does not make mistakes."

"Why does God hate me so much?" I muttered without pulling the covers off my head, "What did I do to deserve this?"

"He doesn't hate you, Abigail," Castiel whispered, "You are precious to Him."

"Then why did he take away my only friend?" I sobbed. "Why did he leave me all alone?"

"It was Danny's time to go," the angel replied, pausing a moment before he added, "And He didn't leave you alone."

Something between a laugh and a sob gurgled up my throat. "Who do I have now?"

"You have me," Castiel murmured, "You have always had me." He let out a slow sigh, perhaps waiting for me to peek my head out from under the blankets or say something back. When I didn't, he cleared his throat and whispered, "I am sorry that I don't have any stories to tell you."

Exhausted from the tears and the trials of the day, I fell asleep soon after his whispered words without ever pulling the covers off my head...

...Muffled laughter drew my thoughts back to the present. Danny and Cassie were carrying on a hushed

conversation while they shared a meal. I could tell by the sounds—the crinkling of fast food wrappers, the telltale crunching noises as they chewed their food—and the smells, which no longer appealed to me in the least. In fact, just the thought of eating turned my stomach.

I tried to listen to what my children were saying, but it was difficult to catch their words because music was playing somewhere in the distance. It must have been coming from the nurse's station down the hall or another patient's room because it was too far-off to make out the lyrics. It was just enough of a distraction to make it difficult to decipher Danny and Cassie's whispered words. I couldn't place the song, but the tune felt familiar.

I fought my way through the opiate-induced fog, concentrating with all my might until I managed to open my eyes.

Danny noticed right away and leaned forward in his chair. "Hey, Mom."

"Hello," I croaked. My throat was so devoid of moisture that it hurt to speak, but I was painfully aware that every coherent moment could be my last with them and I didn't want to waste a single one.

Cassie hopped to her feet and dipped a small sponge at the end of a stick in a cup of water on the bedside table. There were tears in her eyes as she smiled at me and bent down to wet my mouth.

I couldn't even muster the strength to suck the moisture from the sponge, but the discomfort eased a bit as she gently swabbed my tongue.

Danny said something from his seat behind where Cassie was standing, but I couldn't catch his words over the music.

"Do you think you could ask them to turn down that music?" I croaked. "It's hard to hear what you're saying over it."

"What music?" Danny asked as Cassie sat back down beside him. "There isn't any music playing."

"It's distant," I whispered, "maybe coming from another room?"

"We'd hear it better than you if it was coming from another room," Cassie replied in that phony cheerful tone that she always took when she was trying to hide her frustration.

"It's soft," I whispered, "but it's there. Just listen."

Even though his features were a bit of a blur to me, I saw the smile spread across Danny's face. Unlike his sister's forced grin, his was genuine. He understood how precious these last moments were, but Cassie wasn't ready to accept the inevitable just yet. That's why I was hanging on, for her.

"Maybe it's coming from where you're going," Danny whispered.

Despite my fuzzy vision, the scowl that Cassie shot her brother wasn't difficult to see. "What an awful thing to say."

"Why?" Danny whispered as he smiled at me. "I'm not spoiling any surprises. Mom knows she'll be leaving us soon."

Cassie tried to hide the fact that she was wiping tears from the corners of her eyes as she muttered, "Honestly, why can't you be serious?"

"I am being serious," Danny whispered as he winked at me.

A thin wisp of a nurse stepped into the room before Cassie could fire a response back at her brother.

She approached my bedside with a look of compassionate concern and spoke in a low soothing tone, "How are you feeling, Abigail?"

"It hurts," I croaked, feeling guilty for admitting defeat but desperate to dull the pain.

A smile spread across her sweet young face as she whispered, "Well, I can help with that." She ducked out of the room and returned less than a minute later with a syringe in her slender hand.

I smiled at my children to ease their worried expressions as the angel in scrubs stuck the needle in my arm with such expertise that I barely felt it.

Then the world around me slipped away as the music carried me back to the past...

4

"Name"

The Goo Goo Dolls

I weathered more than my fair share of storms over the course of my high school years, and Castiel never failed to visit my dreams after the particularly painful days. In fact, he visited my dreams almost every night for years. My lack of friends during my waking hours began to feel a little less devastating because I had his visits to look forward to at the close of each day...

...It was late on a Friday night at the end of a particularly hellish week of school. I dropped into bed with my phone in hand and my earbuds still in my ears. "Name" by The Goo Goo Dolls, the theme song fate had chosen for me that morning, was playing on repeat. Seconds after my head hit the pillow, the alternative rock band's melancholy tune lulled me off to dreamland.

The angel's visits had become such a routine occurrence that I sensed his presence at the foot of my bed before he uttered a word.

I opened my eyes to greet him with a welcoming smile. "Hello."

"Hello, Abigail," he replied in a hushed tone.

"Name" played softly in the background of my dream as I sat up and frowned at him. "You know, you've never actually told me your name...your *real* name."

"No," he agreed as he stepped up to the side of my bed, "I haven't."

Silly as it was for a loser like me to pity a celestial being, I couldn't help feeling sorry for him. "That just doesn't seem fair to you."

He cocked his head to one side and narrowed his eyes at me. "What makes you say that?"

"Well, you know my name and my face," I whispered, "but I don't know what you actually look like, or even what your name really is. Doesn't that bother you?"

He shook his head as he sat down on the edge of my mattress. "No, it doesn't."

A sympathetic grin spread across my face. "But you aren't going to tell me why it doesn't bother you, are you?"

"It is not a conversation that we are meant to have." He smiled at me as he met my eyes, but the sorrowful blue eyes staring back at me suddenly seemed ancient, as if they bore the wisdom of more centuries than I could ever fathom.

I desperately wanted to believe that he was offering me a subtle glimpse of the real him, but it seemed far more likely that the slip was unintentional. "Why not?"

He dropped his eyes to my hand as he took it in his, flooding my insides with warmth. "I am meant to be your guide here on earth, Abigail. My task is to lead you down the path to eternal salvation. Our relationship is unusual as it is. Guardians do not normally reveal themselves to the humans they watch over."

"Guardians," I muttered, delighting in the feel of the word on my tongue, "So, you really are my guardian angel?"

"Yes," he whispered with a smile that all but melted my heart, "I thought that much was obvious."

A hushed burst of laughter escaped my mouth as I shook my head. "Most people would say the only obvious explanation is that I've lost my mind."

"Fortunately, I am not a person," he whispered as he gave my hand an affectionate squeeze, "and I can tell you with absolute certainty that most people claim to believe that because it is the most acceptable explanation to offer another human. In truth, most humans harbor a deep desire to connect with their spiritual guardian."

I mulled that over for a few seconds before asking, "Do all guardian angels visit their humans in dreams?"

"Many do," he replied with a nod, "but most humans forget their visits when they wake."

My heart ached at the thought of forgetting my nightly visits from Castiel. *Why would God condemn his angels to such a lonely existence?* "Is that the angel's choice, or the human's?"

"It can be either," he whispered, "However, the reason is almost always the same. Most humans simply can't accept the truth. They are afraid to believe in anything that they can't see or touch."

"Then why do I remember your visits when I wake up?"

"Because you are willing," he replied matter-of-factly, "and I want you to."

A dopey grin spread across my face, and I felt like an idiot for not being able to suppress it. "You do?"

He smiled at me, but I caught another flickering glimpse of that ancient sorrow in his eyes. "Yes."

The sorrow in his eyes brought tears to mine as I muttered, "Then why don't you want me to know your real name, or see your true face?"

"It isn't that I do not want that," he replied with an apologetic frown, "It's that it just is not done."

"Revealing your face," I whispered as a tear slid down my cheek, "or your name?"

"Revealing either." He released my hand and brushed the tear from my cheek with his fingertips, warming me with his comforting touch. "You are meant to believe that I am real without concrete proof."

For some stupid reason, my heart ached at his answer. "Then can I give you a name?"

"I already have a name," he replied with a melancholy smile.

"I wish you would share it with me."

That ancient grief flared in his eyes again. "One day, I will."

I felt like a pathetic fool for having such an emotional reaction to his words, but I couldn't help it. It all just felt so terribly unfair. "When?"

His sorrowful smile widened. "When it is time."

There was an inescapable waver to my voice as I asked, "Time for me to *go*?"

"Yes."

"I feel like that should terrify me," I muttered, "but it doesn't. Why is that?"

"Because," he replied in a gruff whisper, "you trust that you will not be alone."

"You say that you don't know any stories," I whispered with a tearful smile, "but it sure feels like you have a story to tell."

"Perhaps." His eyes dropped to my hand as he took it in his again. "But now is not the time to share it."

5

"Hallelujah"
Jeff Buckley

By the grace of God, I made it through those painful solitary years. Little by little, I outgrew my lanky awkwardness and my acne cleared up. As I grew older, I came to recognize the visits from my guardian angel for what they truly were—wishful thinking from a desperate, delusional young girl who needed somebody to comfort her and assure her that she wasn't worthless—but that clarity of thought didn't come for quite some time. In fact, it didn't come at all on my own.

Halfway through my senior year of high school, I joined the youth choir at our church where I was able to revisit my love of singing in a far less toxic environment. Plenty of other misfit teens took solace in the group, and we naturally banded together to form a makeshift herd and protect ourselves from the schoolyard predators. It was wonderful to have friends to sit with at lunch and talk to in the morning before the first bell rang, but the main reason I looked forward to the youth choir meetings was Michael.

Michael was a math teacher in his early twenties and in his spare time, he was also the volunteer director of our parish youth choir. A few weeks after I joined the choir, Michael asked for a volunteer to help him put the room back in order after we were done using it one evening. Since no one else raised their hand, I volunteered because I thought it might be nice to make myself useful for once.

It wasn't long before I started staying late to help with cleanup after every meeting. Michael had this easy going way about him that made conversation feel effortless, and there was a kindness to his smile that made me feel like I could trust him with anything. Our alone time after practice became something that I looked forward to each week. I don't think it took him long to figure out that I was a bit troubled, but he didn't push me to tell him about it. He just casually offered to lend an ear if I ever needed someone to talk to. Desperate for comfort and guidance, I started to open up and share my story with him. Eventually, I even trusted him enough to tell him about Castiel's visits to my dreams. He didn't make me feel foolish for it, but he did help me realize that those visits were a coping mechanism I'd adopted to get myself through the troubled times of my younger years.

Between my new group of friends from the choir and my weekly conversations with Michael, I'd been doing so well that Castiel hadn't paid me a visit in months. But the night after I opened up to Michael about the angel's visits to my dreams, I crawled into bed with Jeff Buckley's version of "Hallelujah" playing on repeat, and I woke to find Castiel standing at the foot of my bed.

I recognized the angel's visit for what it was now, an incredibly vivid dream. In fact, I suspected Castiel's coincidental visit was my mind's way of letting go of a coping mechanism I no longer needed. Whatever the reason for his visit was, I was glad to see his face again.

There was a sharpened intensity to his stare as he met my eyes and murmured, "Hello, Abigail." If I didn't know better, I might have said he looked hurt that I'd pushed him away.

His unbroken eye contact—that so perfectly mimicked the television angel's—made my heart ache. I felt foolish for reacting that way, but there's no controlling what you feel in a dream. "Hi, Castiel. It's uh," I cleared my throat as I searched for words, "It's been a while."

"Yes, it has," he agreed without easing up on his relentless stare.

I dropped my eyes to the collar of his trench coat to escape the fervor in his eyes. "I wasn't sure I would ever see you again."

"I knew you wanted distance," he replied in a gruff whisper.

Distance. That's exactly what Michael had suggested I needed when I opened up to him. "But," I swallowed the lump in my throat, "you're here now."

He took a single step toward me as he nodded. "Yes, I am."

I exhaled an unsteady breath and lifted my eyes to meet his gaze. *Why did my imaginary angel's stare have the power to affect me this deeply?* "Is that all you're going to say?"

He narrowed his eyes at me as he took another step. "Would you like me to say more?"

Lost in the depths of his ancient blue eyes, I cleared my throat as I struggled to find my voice. "I don't know."

"You should keep your distance from the choir director too," my angel replied with an apologetic frown.

An ache flared in my chest as I muttered, "Michael?"

Castiel's unyielding stare continued to hold me captive as he nodded.

"Why?" I whispered in a small uncertain voice.

"The thoughts in his head are not pure," my angel replied matter-of-factly.

A rush of heat burned my cheeks, but I forced myself to keep holding his gaze. "How would you—"

"Trust me, Abigail," he interrupted in a harsh whisper, "Even if you no longer believe that I am real, trust what I am telling you now."

"But this is just a dream," I muttered, "None of this has ever been real."

A regretful smile tugged at the corners of his mouth. "I understand that you need to believe that now, but I am asking you to trust me on this anyway."

For no logical reason that I could come up with, my eyes filled with tears.

The angel's eyes did the same. "Remember this conversation, Abigail."

The dream ended abruptly with a quiet swish of his wings as he vanished from my room, but I never forgot his words.

Silly as it might have been to put such trust in advice I received from a fictional character in a dream, I told Michael that I couldn't help with cleanup anymore at the next meeting; and I was careful never to spend time alone with him again...

...The music was louder now. It was odd, how familiar the tune seemed, since I still couldn't place the song. It was a lovely tune that saddened me while simultaneously filling me with joy.

It was easier to open my eyes this time because the pain was more intense. The ache cleared my head and helped anchor me to the present.

The room was much darker now, and Danny was the only one with me. He was asleep, slumped in a cushioned chair that he'd slid up close to my bedside.

I didn't want to wake him because I knew how exhausting this whole ordeal had been for him. He'd barely left my side for more than a few hours at a time for God only knew how many days. I had lost all track of how much time had passed since they'd moved me into this sterile room to die.

As I laid there watching my son sleep, the music grew a bit louder. The joy that the tune evoked was indescribable. It warmed my old heart and brought tears to my failing eyes. Yet, I still couldn't place the song.

As much as I wanted to stay with Danny, the music washed over me and carried me back to the past...

... College was much easier for me than high school had ever been. I made new friends and Castiel stopped visiting my dreams altogether; but television remained a welcome reprieve from my reality, especially *Supernatural*. Whenever I watched Sam, Dean and Castiel battle the evil in their world, I could lose myself in their fight to survive and forget about my own troubles for a while. I wouldn't have admitted it to anyone, but in those blissful moments, I still imagined a world where those beautiful men had my back. I would've given just about anything to have a guardian angel like Castiel watching over me for real.

I'd never done any drinking during my high school days—mostly because I had no friends to drink with—but college was a different story. It didn't take long for me to discover a whole new reprieve from what ailed me. The haziness that alcohol brought on dulled all my old hurts; and being the timid creature that I was, the loss of inhibitions that accompanied the haze was a welcome bonus.

Looking back on it, I realize how stupid I was. A naïve innocent little thing like myself was just begging for trouble, drinking massive amounts of alcohol in the company of drunken college boys. Once again, my final hours lifted the veil of ignorance that had clouded my view of another possible moment of divine intervention in my past...

...I had only gone out drinking a handful of times, to keg parties with a big group of friends, but this night was different. Our posse for the evening consisted of nothing more than three fresh-faced girls, who might as well have had *naïve virgin* tattooed across their foreheads. We were at a frat house party but this fraternity was new to us, and so were the shots of cheap vodka that they were serving along with the beer.

The memory was hazy for obvious reasons, but I remembered meeting a couple of freshman boys, new faces that I couldn't have identified in a lineup the next day if my life depended on it. I think one of them was Asian and the other one had light brown hair, but I couldn't even say that with any certainty. We all started downing shots together, and somehow—in the midst of all the alcohol-induced haziness—one of the boys' lips ended up colliding with mine. Damned if I could even remember which of the two boys it was, but damaged as I was from all the bullying I'd endured in my younger years, my drunken-self delighted in the fact that *any* boy would take such an interest in me.

When I pulled my lips away from the boy's, the music was deafening, the room was a blur and my friends were nowhere in sight. Too drunk to feel anything more than mildly uneasy with my current situation, I searched the crowd of blurry faces for the familiar ones I'd come to the party with. But the boy took me by the hand as he murmured in my ear, telling me not to worry while he gently tugged me across the crowded room.

I don't even recall exactly how it happened, but the next thing I knew a much older boy with the fraternity's letters on his baseball cap and hoodie was towering over me. He bent his head close to my ear so I could hear him over the blaring music. "You're drunk."

I grinned up at him like an idiot without a care in the world. "I know."

"I'm taking you home now," he declared in no uncertain terms.

His statement made me feel a bit uncomfortable, but I was too intoxicated to be overly concerned by it. In my altered state, it never even occurred to me that I had any say in the matter as I parroted his words back to him in an unsteady voice, "You're taking me home?"

"I'm taking you to *your* home," he clarified, with his mouth close to my ear.

The next thing I remember, I was on a campus transport bus sitting next to the tall upperclassman, who was really much more man than boy. The man-boy confided that his girlfriend was pissed off at him for leaving the party to babysit some random drunken freshman girl, but he said he wouldn't have been able to forgive himself if he hadn't stepped in when he did. Looking back on it with a sober adult mind, I shuddered to think how that night could have turned out if he hadn't intervened.

I ended that blurry night with a spinning head back in my dorm room, where I passed out safe and sound in my own bed.

Like the two freshman boys at the party, I could never have identified that senior frat brother who took it upon himself to watch out for me that night. I could've bumped into him on campus the very next day and never even recognized him. *What exactly had compelled him to leave the party that night for a stupid drunken freshman he'd never even met before?* I would never know for sure, but once again in retrospect it felt like someone had been watching out for me that night. Looking back on it now, I couldn't help wondering if a subliminal nudge from a celestial being might have prompted that knight-in-shining-Greek-letters to get me out of harm's way...

...The song sounded clearer now, but I still couldn't make out the words. The pain medication—or perhaps the cancer—was jumbling my thoughts. Whatever song it was, it was a lovely tune. The singer had a beautiful voice and I knew in my heart that this song surpassed all others for some inexplicable reason.

As I opened my eyes, Danny smiled at me from his contorted position in the cushioned chair beside my bed. If I were to twist my limbs like that, I would never be able to right them again. But my Danny endured the discom-fort because he didn't want to miss a moment of time that could be spent with me.

I smiled back at him despite the pain. "You really can't hear the music?"

His smile widened as he shook his head. "Nope, not at all."

"It's louder now," I muttered, "like the source is getting nearer."

He sat up and dropped his shoeless feet to the floor. "Would I know the song?"

"I'm not sure," I muttered, "I am almost positive I should know it myself, but I can't quite place it."

He propped his head up with a fist, displaying a hopelessly mussed-up head of hair. "Is it a good song?"

"It's glorious," I whispered in a thicker voice, "but I'm not exactly sure why."

A conspiratorial grin lit up his face. "I still think it's coming from where you're headed."

"You shouldn't antagonize your sister," I whispered, though I couldn't even feign a look of disapproval.

He let out a whispered chuckle. "She just makes it so darn easy."

"Be good to each other after I'm gone," I muttered in a broken whisper.

"You know we will," he answered as he reached out and took my hand. *"You taught us well, Mom."*

Suddenly, the notion of leaving my children behind seemed unbearable. A tear slid down my cheek as I whispered, *"I certainly tried my best."*

"You did amazing," he whispered. *"That's something even Cassie and I can agree on.*

6

"Just Breathe"
Pearl Jam

I'd like to say that my college years made me wiser, but that wouldn't be entirely true. Sure, I gained plenty of book smarts, but that's not the sort of wisdom I'm referring to. The ability to make intelligent life choices isn't something you can learn from books.

Collin didn't really start out as a bad choice. He was a pretty face with a breathtaking stare and a mischievous smile that I fell for almost instantly...

...It was two weeks into the fall semester of my junior year, and I was at a keg party with a group of my girlfriends. If there was one lesson that we'd all learned by our junior year, it was to stick together and watch each other's backs when we went out drinking. I may not have been a genius when it came to street smarts, but I'd definitely learned my lesson the night the man-boy saved my ass at the frat party my freshman year. I'd had plenty of time to think my actions over the next morning while I was puking my guts out, terrified to think of what could have happened to me because of my stupidity. From there on out, my friends and I went to parties in a tight pack and we kept each other in sight to prevent any of us from making regrettable intoxicated decisions.

This night started out just like any other college party night. The music was blaring, there were red plastic cups in every hand and tipsy girls were gyrating on the makeshift dance floor in the frat house living room. My group stood together in a corner by the door, watching the drunken dancers in the center of the room writhe to the music while we waited for the beer to kick in enough to join them.

I hadn't thought about the playlist that Danny had made for me in ages. The pain of losing my friend was an old ache that I'd learned to avoid tweaking with painful reminders, the way a retired ball player learns to favor a once injured limb. I was half-listening to my friends' conversation as I downed the liquid courage in my cup, anxious to shed my inhibitions and get out on the dance floor.

As my eyes wandered over the sea of intoxicated dancers, a boy across the room caught my eye. He was gorgeous—not much taller than me but with a solid athletic build, purposely mussed-up hair and a stare that made me go weak at the knees—and *he was staring at me*. How on earth I managed to catch this boy's eye, I would never know; but there was no mistaking the fact that his eyes were fixed on me.

As I stood there staring back at him over the lip of my red plastic cup, Pearl Jam's "Just Breathe," the sixth song on Danny's playlist, started playing.

And time stopped.

My inebriated brain took the song as a sign from Danny. He was sending me a message and I wasn't about to ignore him. My childhood friend had never gotten the chance to catch a gorgeous stranger's eye across a crowded dance floor. I owed it to Danny not to waste this opportunity. For him, I vowed to savor this night and be grateful that I was alive to enjoy it.

I downed what little beer I had left, then traced my lips with the tip of my tongue as I lowered the cup from my mouth without shying away from the boy's stare for a second.

The boy started toward me as he hungrily watched me trace my lips with the tip of my tongue, almost as if I'd inadvertently stumbled upon some sort of secret frat party mating call. I felt my face flush but I continued to hold his stare, luring him closer with my unwitting spell.

He stepped right up to our group of friends without the slightest bit of hesitation over approaching a tight pack of the opposite sex. In fact, he acted as if no one existed in that room but the two of us. His eyes didn't stray from mine for even a second to check out the girls I was with.

"Just Breathe" seemed to swell in the background, as if Danny were reminding me to relax and take a breath. It was a necessary reminder because the intensity of this boy's stare at close range took my breath away.

He put a hand on my waist and leaned in close to my ear to be heard above the music. "You need another drink?" Such unremarkable first words to utter and yet, my aged brain still remembered them with crystal clarity.

Emboldened by the alcohol that was coursing through my bloodstream, I leaned against his solid frame as I lifted my lips to his ear and answered in a throaty whisper, "Yeah, I think I do."

He turned his head and smiled at me, and my limbs turned to jelly. Thank goodness he'd slipped his arm more securely around my waist when I leaned into him. If he hadn't, I'm not sure I would've managed to stay upright. He tipped his head and touched his forehead to the side of my head as he brought his lips to my ear again, caressing the flesh of my earlobe with the warmth of his breath as he murmured, "Come on then."

This was nothing like that night during my freshman year when the frat brother had felt the need to swoop in and come to my rescue. I didn't want anyone to rescue me from this boy. He could have led me anywhere with that muscular arm around my waist, and I would've gone willingly. Somehow, my friends must have sensed that because none of them said a word as the boy swept me away by the waist.

He weaved his way through the crowded dance floor, parting the crowd with the sheer intensity of his stare and sweeping me right along with him till we made our way into the kitchen. There was a line of party-goers mingling with their empty cups in hand as they waited for more beer, but they parted for him just like the people on the dance floor had. As we stepped up to the frat brother who was filling empty cups, the boy took mine from my hand and held it out to him.

As the frat brother filled my cup, the boy dipped his head and brought his mouth close to my ear again, despite the fact that the music wasn't all that loud in the kitchen. "I'm Collin, by the way."

I took the cup from the frat brother with an appreciative nod. As Collin held his empty cup out for a refill, I turned my head and smiled up at him.

God he was beautiful. If this was a dream, I just prayed that I wouldn't wake up too soon. "I'm Abigail," I replied in a seductive murmur fueled by the liquid courage, "but my friends call me Abbie."

"Abigail," he replied in a rough whisper as he took his cup from the frat brother without taking his eyes off of me for a second. "I don't think I want to be your friend."

A stupid grin spread across my face as he led me back out of the kitchen. "Good."

We weaved our way through the crowd to the front door, and I followed him through it without any hesitation. Wherever he planned to take me, I wanted to go.

But he didn't take me far. There was an unoccupied couch with beer-stained cushions off to one side of the front porch. He maneuvered us to it and sat us both down without taking his arm from my waist. It was an early autumn night and the temperature was mild enough, but a slight breeze danced through my hair and sent a shiver down my spine.

He tightened his hold on my waist, sliding me closer to him. "I thought it would be easier to talk out here, but we can go back in if you're too cold."

"No, this is good," I murmured, leaning into the warmth of his body. "So, are you some sort of campus celebrity or something?"

His mischievous grin was far more intoxicating than the drink in my hand. "What makes you ask that?"

I bit my lip to suppress a shiver that had nothing to do with the breeze. "How come you don't have to wait in line for a drink like the rest of us?"

His throaty chuckle heated my insides. *How on earth had I snagged this boy's attention?* "It's just one of the many perks of being a brother in his senior year."

"Huh," I muttered, "This is your fraternity?"

"So, Abigail," he replied with a dismissive nod, as if the topic of his fraternity was of no interest to him, "how long do we have before your friends come out and try to steal you away from me?"

I was midway through a sip of beer, and a giggle that I couldn't fully contain almost made me choke on it. "Is it that obvious that we travel in a pack?"

He sat his drink down on the floor of the porch then took the cup from my hand and set it down next to his. "Yeah, kinda."

"It didn't seem like you noticed my friends," I murmured as his eyes locked with mine.

"That was the idea," he replied in a husky whisper as he pulled me closer, "No eye contact, no dirty looks."

I let out a hushed giggle. "Were they giving you dirty looks?"

"Don't know," he whispered in my ear, lightly brushing his lips against my earlobe as he spoke, "I couldn't take my eyes off of you."

No longer the least bit chilled by the breeze, I smiled at him as he lowered his lips to mine. I had kissed more than a few boys by this point in my college career, but no other set of lips had ever affected me like his.

The world around us—the frat house, the muffled music wafting out from inside, the porch and even the couch we were sitting on—all of it melted away as he crushed his lips against mine in a possessive, passionate, toe-curling kiss...

...The aches in my body wrenched me away from the memory far too soon. Even now—after all these years— as I lay on my deathbed with my body growing colder by the hour, the memory of that kiss warmed me.

The pain was much more intense now. Hard as I tried, I couldn't muster the strength to open my eyes or utter a sound. All I could do was pray for somebody to make it stop.

It won't last much longer, Abigail. I promise. It will all be over soon, **a voice whispered inside my head.**

Tears streamed down my cheeks as I focused on the warmth of that voice.

Someone brushed the tears from my cheeks and spoke to me in a hushed tone, but I was too far gone to recognize his voice or comprehend the meaning of his words.

7

"Have You Ever Seen the Rain"
Creedence Clearwater Revival

Creedence Clearwater Revival's "Have You Ever Seen the Rain" had been stuck in my head since I'd pulled Danny's playlist up on my phone earlier that morning and put it on shuffle. My randomly chosen theme song for the day seemed fitting, given the black cloud that was hanging over me, threatening to rain on my happiness. It was a gorgeous day. The sun was shining in a cloudless blue sky. The air was warm, and Collin and I didn't have a care in the world. Finals were over and graduation was only a few days away.

We sat on a blanket that he kept in the trunk of his car, for just this sort of impromptu occasion, eating a cold fast-food lunch by the lake. We were the only souls on the secluded stretch of beach, and we'd been taking full advantage of the privacy for the past couple hours while our forgotten picnic grew cold.

Collin tossed his half-eaten burger aside and smiled at me as he pulled me into his arms. "You know, I'm really not that hungry. What do you say we go back to what we were doing before?"

I dropped the fry in my hand to the grass as I slid onto his lap and kissed him.

After a few blissful minutes, he broke the kiss and leaned back to look me in the eye. "God, I wish I could stop time."

"I know," I murmured, "I'm not sure how I'm going to survive without you next year."

He lazily traced a finger along my jawline as he whispered, "What if you didn't have to?"

When he leaned in to kiss me again, I pulled my head back and muttered, "What do you mean?"

The affectionate grin that spread across his face melted my insides. "Come with me."

"I can't do that," I muttered, ignoring the butterflies that took flight in my stomach at his words, "I have another year of school to finish and—"

"They have schools in New York," he countered, cutting my flimsy excuse off at the knees.

"Be serious." I narrowed my eyes at him, sizing him up as I tried to determine whether he *was* being serious. "Where would I stay?"

"My apartment," he paused to steal a kiss before adding, "We've practically been living together for the past year, Abigail. My frat brothers treat you like a member of the family."

"Playing house is a lot different from actually moving into an apartment together."

"I know that." He turned me sideways on his lap, so he could look me in the eye. "I'm tired of playing. Come live with me in New York."

I wanted to say yes so badly it hurt. Of course, I knew there had to be plenty of logical reasons why I shouldn't but for the life of me, I couldn't come up with a single one. "I can't just pick up and move away from my mom."

He raised a questioning eyebrow. "Does your mother make you happy?"

My mother had made me feel like a nuisance for as long as I could remember; but when I was with Collin, I almost believed I was worth something. I swallowed the lump in my throat and muttered, "You know she doesn't."

"Then to hell with her," he whispered, "Come live with me, and let yourself be happy."

I exhaled a pent-up sigh as a logical reason *not* to move across the country with him occurred to me. "What happens when you get tired of me or you meet somebody better?"

He brushed a stray strand of hair back from my face and tucked it behind my ear. "Don't do that."

I touched my forehead to his and whispered, "Don't do what?"

"Doubt how much I love you," he murmured as his eyes locked with mine.

"I'm just being realistic," I replied in a broken whisper as I pulled my head back from his, "You'll constantly be surrounded by beautiful people working in the music business."

Collin studied me through narrowed eyes as he murmured, "Why can't you see how beautiful the face staring back at you in the mirror is?"

"I think you should get your eyes checked," I muttered, "You're in serious need of some glasses."

"Stop it," he whispered, "Don't put down the girl I love."

"She doesn't deserve you," I muttered as I dropped my eyes to the collar of his shirt, "You could do better."

He dipped his head at an awkward angle to look me in the eye. "I love you, Abigail. Hell, I'd ask you to marry me today if I thought you were ready for that. I know you're not, but don't doubt how much I love you."

An involuntary smile spread across my face at his words. "What did I ever do to deserve you?"

"I should be asking *you* that question," he whispered.

I shook my head and bit my lip to keep my eyes from tearing.

"Come with me," he murmured close to my ear.

I dropped my head to his shoulder and squeezed my eyes shut, wishing with all my heart that I could stop time and just stay in this perfect moment.

He wrapped his arms around me and kissed the top of my head. "Is that a yes?"

"Yeah," I whispered, "I think it is."

"Have You Ever Seen the Rain" was still playing softly in my head as Collin lowered me to the blanket and covered my lips with his…

…There were more voices in the room now but they were growing fainter, and I had no idea what they were saying or even whose voices they were.

The pain was excruciating and I needed it to stop.

You don't have to stay here, **a voice whispered inside my head.** *Let go, and I will take you away right now. You've lived a good life, Abigail. It's time for you to say goodbye.*

I wanted to let go, but I heard my Cassie's tearful voice rise above the others in the room. She wasn't ready to let me go yet. I had to stay until she was. *I can't. My daughter still needs me.*

A hand stroked the side of my face as the music grew louder, drowning out all the voices in the room. *She will be alright, Abigail. You don't have to keep suffering like this.*

I focused on the warmth that flooded through me as the hand brushed across my cheek. *Will you stay with me?*

I have never left you, Abigail.

8

"White Rabbit"
Jefferson Airplane

Life in New York was great in the beginning. Collin's career at the recording company seemed like a gift from God. His salary was partially dependent on commissions, and with his commanding presence and charming good looks, it wasn't long before he was making enough to pay for our trendy apartment in the city and help me out with my school payments.

Unfortunately, all the wining and dining that Collin was expected to do with his clients didn't exactly encourage him to stop drinking and partying like a frat boy. Don't get me wrong, he wasn't unfaithful to me or anything like that. He just wanted me to come out and party with him almost every night. It was amazing at first. We ate like kings, drank like fish and made love like bunnies, and I still managed to get decent grades in school. In fact, I didn't really see any problem with the way things were until the night we ended up at a party at his boss's penthouse apartment...

...I was comfortably tucked away on a plush couch in a corner of the crowded room, slowly nursing my fourth gin and tonic. The room was starting to spin because I hadn't eaten much, and I was thinking about how I really should be getting home to study for the exam I had to take in the morning. The other party-goers who were seated in my little corner of the room were deeply engrossed in a conversation that didn't interest me in the slightest. I smiled or nodded every now and then when it seemed appropriate, but paid little attention to what they were saying.

Collin was seated at a table across the room, talking shop with his boss and the musical guest of honor for the evening. Every so often, he would look my way and flash me a smile that left me aching to get home so I could have him all to myself.

As they all stood up from the table, the ear-to-ear grin on Collin's face was the only subtle sign that he was sloshed. He sauntered across the room straight and steady, and took a seat beside me on the couch.

"Oh, come on," his boss muttered under his breath as he watched Collin sit back and wrap an arm around me. Collin's boss was a far more obvious drunk. He slurred his words when he spoke, swayed when he walked and openly ogled anything in a skirt without regard to their age, availability, or interest in him.

Collin grinned at his boss as he took the drink I'd been nursing out of my hand and downed a sizable swig. "You got something to say, Kurt?"

"The night is young," his boss murmured as his eyes raked over me, "It's too early for you two to curl up on the couch like an old married couple. Work is over. Let's have some fun."

The scowl on Collin's face, as he eyed Kurt and shook his head, clearly conveyed his displeasure with his boss's wandering eyes. "I think we're good right here."

"Fair enough," his boss muttered. With that, he turned his back to us and swerved his way toward the bar at the other end of the room. He ducked behind it for a few seconds, then gripped the edge of the bar to steady himself as he stood back up with a tin box tucked under one arm. There was a lopsided grin on his face as he swerved his way back across the crowded room.

Kurt's eyes fixed on me as he sat down on the coffee table in front of us. "You ever try anything stronger than alcohol, sweetheart?"

Collin had smoked pot every now and then during his fraternity days, but I'd never had any interest in trying that or any other mind-altering substance beyond a stiff drink. My stomach turned as Collin's boss opened the box and pulled out a plastic baggie full of white powder and a small bundle of short straws.

A low growl emanated from Collin's throat. "If you think I'm letting you get us wasted so you can screw my girlfriend, you're out of your damn mind."

Collin's crude words and menacing tone, Kurt's lecherous stare and my queasy stomach—combined with the obscene amount of alcohol coursing through our collective bloodstreams—felt like a sure recipe for disaster. Eager to avoid causing a scene, I turned toward my boyfriend and leaned in close to his ear. "Just take me home, Collin."

"Relax, babe." He pulled me flush against his side and planted a rough kiss on my cheek. "Nobody's gonna make you do anything that you don't want to do."

Kurt let out an inebriated chuckle as he dumped a bit of powder from the plastic bag onto the glass tabletop beside where he was seated. His eyes returned to me as he fumbled to extract his wallet from his back pocket without standing up. He winked at me as he slipped a credit card out of the wallet.

Then he turned his attention to the table as he used the edge of the card to rake the powder into a couple of neat white lines. He pulled his head back and studied his handiwork with a nod of satisfaction. Then he fixed his eyes on Collin. "How about you, tough guy? Are you too whipped to step up and play with the big boys tonight?"

Collin glared at his boss as he downed what was left of my drink and sat the empty glass on the end table beside him. "Piss off."

A mischievous grin spread across Kurt's face as his eyes shifted to me. "Is this innocent act of his fooling you, sweetheart? Don't let your boyfriend dupe you into thinking he's never partaken in anything stronger than alcohol. He's just playing nice because you're here. So, why not have a little fun tonight and let your man off the leash to indulge like he normally would?"

Heat rushed to my face as I turned to Collin and waited for him to say it wasn't true.

But he didn't.

Never one to back down from a challenge, especially when under the influence, Collin snatched one of the straws from Kurt's hand with an irritated growl. Then he lowered his head to the lines of powder on the tabletop as he muttered, "Leave her out of this, asshole." With that, he plugged one nostril and inhaled the line of powder that was closest to him up the other nostril with the straw.

My nausea intensified as I watched my boyfriend take a quick deep sniff, shake his head, then repeat the whole process—snorting the remaining line of powder up his other nostril—with an ease that suggested this was nothing new to him.

"Collin," I muttered, "I think we should go home now."

"Don't be a buzzkill, sweetheart," his boss murmured as he dumped a bit more powder from the bag onto the table and formed two more neat lines, "Loosen up and let your boy have some fun. Why not give it a try before you go snapping the whip and judging all of us?"

Tears stung my eyes but I blinked them back, unwilling to show weakness in front of all these people. Suppressing the hurt that I felt spurred a momentary flashback—to all those nightmarish encounters with schoolyard predators in my younger days—and all the old sensations of helplessness and humiliation came rushing back to me as the taste of bile burned its way up my throat. "I've got a test in the morning," I muttered as I turned to Collin. "You can stay, but I'm getting out of here. I'll call a cab."

I stood up from the couch, but Collin gripped my wrist as I started to walk away. "Come on. Don't leave me sitting here all alone like a chump."

"He won't be alone," a leggy blond on the couch across from us assured me in a throaty rasp. "I'll keep him company after you're gone."

The room spun around us as Collin tightened his grip on my wrist, and I forgot how to breathe. I'd uprooted my life and moved across the country for this man, and I apparently didn't have a clue who he was anymore. *If Collin had hidden the fact that he was doing drugs, what other secrets was he keeping from me?* Too stunned to speak, I just blinked at the leggy blond.

"Or you could stay," she murmured with a seductive wink, "and we can *all* have some fun."

I felt desperate to get out of that apartment. I needed air, and I needed a strong pair of arms to wrap around me and make it all better. But the man I always turned to for support had morphed into a stranger when I wasn't looking. "I've gotta go," I muttered, "I have a test in the morning and—"

"Walk with me," Collin interrupted as he stood up from the couch without loosening his grip on my wrist.

Before I could even come up with a response, he was tugging me across the crowded room and maneuvering us down an empty hallway.

We stopped at the far end of the hall, but in my disoriented daze it felt like the hallway kept moving. "What's going on?" I whimpered as the world spun around us, "Who are you?"

"You know who I am," he whispered close to my ear, "Nothing's changed. I've got a certain image I need to maintain with this crowd, but that's just part of my job. I'm still the same guy who fell head over heels in love with you the minute I spotted you across a crowded room at that frat party back in college."

"I thought you were," I muttered in an unsteady voice, "but you've obviously been keeping things from me. *College-you* would never have done that."

"I have to keep up appearances now," he murmured, "I didn't mention the coke because I don't do it that often and I didn't want to worry you over nothing, but I don't want to keep anything from you anymore. I want you to be a part of all of it from now on."

I squeezed my eyes shut to stop the room from spinning, but the motion was even worse with my eyes closed. "What does that even mean?"

He exhaled a long deep sigh that sent a shiver racing down my spine. "Play along with me at parties. Help me play the part, and nothing has to change for us the rest of the time."

I shook my head, but quickly regretted it when it amplified my wooziness. "Play along *how*?"

"Give it a try, just this once," he murmured as he pulled me closer. "Then I'll sneak you off to an empty room and make love to you while we're both flying high. I want us to plunge over the edge of the world together, just once. If you don't like it, I'll never ask again…and I'll stop doing it too."

I opened my eyes and locked them with his. The world was still spinning around us, and the music suddenly seemed way too loud. *I felt so lost.* Collin had healed so much of what I thought would be broken inside me forever. *Was his request really all that unreasonable?* If I tried it and told him I didn't like it, then that would be the end of it and we could both move on.

The frantic tune blaring down the hall from the other room faded away as the song came to an end, and I drew a deep breath in that brief respite from the noise.

I recognized the seductive beat of "White Rabbit" by Jefferson Airplane the moment it started playing. It was the eighth song on Danny's playlist. Once again, it felt like Danny was stepping in from beyond the grave to guide me down the right path. It seemed fitting, considering the fact that it was a song from Danny's playlist that'd bolstered my confidence the night I first saw Collin across that crowded room. But what exactly was Danny trying to tell me this time? *Give in to my boyfriend's request, or get the hell out of there?*

Sensing my internal conflict, Collin pulled me closer and drew me into a deep passionate kiss.

I willingly let him back me against the wall because the room was still spinning and my legs were on the verge of buckling. *What was I so afraid of?* It was only one time. I should just do this for Collin because he'd done so much for me.

"I promise you," Collin rasped as he broke the kiss, "It'll be incredible. Free-fall with me with our senses heightened just this once, and I swear to God you'll hear the angels sing."

Angels. A vision of Castiel—*my* Castiel—came to mind at the mention of angels and with that image, came a single spoken word in my dream angel's deep voice. *Don't.*

This was wrong. I knew I should just leave the party.

"Just once," Collin whispered as "White Rabbit" blared from down the hall, "and if you don't like it, we'll never do it again."

Castiel's voice sounded in my head again. *Don't, Abigail.*

"If I don't like it," I muttered, ignoring my angel's words of warning, "then that will be the end of it...for both of us?"

Collin nodded. "I promise you. If you don't like it, I'll never bring it up again."

There was only one problem with that, one that my altered mind never anticipated.

I *did* like it...

...How long had I been like this?

I was floating, detached from the physical world as I listened to their muffled voices echoing from far away.

Their words had lost all meaning to me. Everything just felt so chaotic and foreign now. I didn't belong there anymore...in that body...with those people... in that world. The only thing that was still tethering me to that plane of existence was my daughter's stubborn refusal to let me go.

*She will be alright, Abigail, **the voice inside my head assured me.** Your son will take good care of her after you're gone. They'll get through this together. You don't have to endure any more of this pain.*

I tried to shake my head, but I didn't seem to have any control over the movement of my body. I can't go until Cassie lets me know that she'll be okay without me.

There was no response, only that music far off in the distance that remained unknown to me despite how familiar it felt...

9

"Why Should I Cry for You?"

Sting

L eaving Collin was the hardest decision I'd ever had to make. That's why I waited so much longer than I should have to end it—that, plus the fact that I couldn't quite embrace the idea of kicking my own addiction. I knew it was wrong, but everything just seemed to fall into place when I was flying high with Collin and for those brief moments, *it felt so right.* So I let things drag on long enough for me to fail out of school, and then get fired from the two jobs I managed to get, during the year that Collin and I slipped deeper and deeper into the drug scene.

After I lost the second job, I couldn't deny it any longer. That was no way to live my life. I knew Collin and I would probably both end up living on the street or dead if we continued down the dark path that the two of us had veered onto; but *knowing* that and doing something about it were two very different things.

I took my first step toward getting out the day I finally worked up the nerve to call a drug addiction hotline. The caring voice on the other end of the phone talked with me for over an hour. Then she directed me toward the nearest Narcotics Anonymous meeting place, but it took two more weeks for me to work up the courage to attend a meeting...

...I didn't stand up to speak at that first meeting. It pretty much took all the courage I could muster just to show up, sit in the back row and listen. I had every intention of slipping out the back door and heading home as soon as the meeting ended, but a woman who looked about the same age as my mother approached me before I could reach the door.

"It'll get easier to share your story," she assured me with a kind smile. Something in the woman's eyes convinced me to stay and talk for a minute, and it wasn't just the kindred sorrow. It was the genuine empathy in her gentle brown eyes that kept me rooted where I stood.

"I'm not so sure I want to share my story with all these people," I muttered, "I've never been much of a public speaker."

"You're looking at it all wrong," she replied with a dismissive shake of her head, "Don't think of it as public speaking. Think of it as confiding in a group of friends who understand exactly where you're at right now."

"How could you possibly know where I'm at?" I muttered, wondering whether her presumptuous advice should make me feel insulted, or understood and accepted.

"I've been there," she whispered with a sorrowful smile, "We all have, and we can help you if you let us in. My name is Judy, by the way. What's yours?"

"It's Abigail," I muttered, "and I just came to check out a meeting. I'm not even sure if I'll be coming back."

"Well then, why don't you let me buy you dinner tonight?" she offered, with a casual sort of confidence that I would never have been able to muster for a stranger. *How could she be so sure that I wouldn't just laugh in her face?*

"I don't know," I muttered as I glanced over my shoulder at the door. "I wouldn't feel right about letting you pay for my meal."

"It's no big deal. I own the diner we'd be eating at. Besides, it's sort of a tradition of mine," she added with an undeterred grin, "treating a friend to dinner after her first meeting."

"We aren't friends," I muttered as I took a backward step toward the exit.

"We could be if you let me in," Judy whispered as she touched a hand to my shoulder.

The simple gesture of affection felt odd to me, since it was more than my own mother ever offered. Yet somehow it felt right, like a missing piece of my puzzle had fallen into place...

...Judy and I did share a meal at her diner that night. She kept it very low key and didn't pressure me for any personal details. We mostly chatted about trivial things—our favorite movies, the types of music we liked to listen to—nothing even remotely earth-shattering. It was Judy's casual unassuming kindness that convinced me to go back and attend another meeting the following week. A week after that, Judy became my sponsor.

I didn't tell Collin about the N.A. meetings at first. In fact, I went to the meetings for over a month before I said a word to him about my desire to get clean and turn my life around. When I finally felt strong enough to broach the subject, I begged Collin to come to a meeting with me. But if my drug problem had gotten out of hand, his addiction was nothing short of catastrophic.

Collin wanted nothing to do with drug addiction hotlines or N.A. meetings, and there wasn't a darn thing I could do to change his mind. I did try—for almost a year—but in the end, I had to accept the fact that he didn't want my help and I couldn't stay in such a toxic relationship. What chance did I have of turning my life around if I was still living with an addict?

It wasn't an easy decision. In fact, it was a downright impossible choice. I loved Collin with all my heart, but Judy and the other members of my N.A. group eventually helped me come to grips with what I needed to do. Despite how much I loved him, I couldn't throw the rest of my life away for Collin. So, I moved out of our apartment and stayed with Judy for about a month while I got clean. After that, Judy offered me a job in her diner and a clean place to stay. It was a small apartment a few blocks from her restaurant that she was kind enough to rent to me dirt cheap, and I was deeply grateful to have it.

The plan was to get myself back on my feet and eventually go back and finish college, and things went pretty well for eight months. I worked hard. I scrimped and saved as much money as I could, and I kept my apartment—and my nose—clean. In fact, everything was going so well that I was considering taking a class or two at the local community college in the fall. Then Collin's boss came strolling into the diner on a Tuesday afternoon during the lunchtime rush...

...The bell above the door jingled, announcing the arrival of a new customer, and I turned toward the door just in time to watch Kurt step into the restaurant.

Just the sight of Collin's boss made my stomach clench, as if someone had hauled off and punched me in the gut. A wave of nausea washed over me as I watched him cross the room and sit down at a booth in my section.

I grabbed a menu from the stack, squared my shoulders and took a deep breath as I stepped out from behind the counter. *I could do this.* Kurt played no part in my life now. There wasn't anything that he could do or say that would undo all the progress I'd made.

I plastered a phony customer service smile on my face as I approached his table and handed him the menu. Determined to come across as confident and unfazed by his surprise appearance, I made a conscious effort to keep my voice steady and look him in the eye. "Hello, Kurt. Can I take your drink order?" That's when I finally took a good look at him.

He looked like hell.

His face was pale, dark circles underscored his bloodshot eyes, his clothes were wrinkled, and his hair was a disheveled mess. Tears swam in his eyes as he looked up at me with a vacant stare. "Oh shit," he muttered under his breath, "You, uh...you haven't heard yet, have you?"

My stomach dropped at the pained expression on Kurt's face and for a moment, I actually considered turning around and running away from him. Whatever it was that I hadn't heard, I was pretty sure I wanted to remain in the dark about it. I barely managed to squeak out the words, "Heard what?"

He was silent for so long with such an apprehensive frown on his face that I half expected *him* to get up and run away. "Collin uh," Kurt paused to clear his throat then muttered, "He OD'd two days ago, Abigail."

The contents of my stomach surged as I whispered, "Is he...in the hospital?"

"No." Kurt's eyes dropped to the paper placemat on the table in front of him as he shook his head and muttered, "He's dead."

Dead? That horrid word seemed to suck all the air from the room as the world around me slipped out of focus.

Before I could even process the fact that my legs were giving out, Kurt lunged from the booth, caught me in an awkward grab and pulled me into the booth beside him.

Despite how much I'd always disliked him, I dropped my head to his shoulder and broke down in tears as his arms wrapped around me. "No," I sobbed, "That can't be true."

"I wish it wasn't," Kurt whispered as he grabbed a napkin from the table. For a second, it looked like he meant to wipe the tears from my cheeks. Then he seemed to think better of it and cleared his throat as he held the napkin out to me...

...Faint hospital sounds began to mingle with the idle chatter of the lunchtime rush, drowning out the customers' voices as the heart-wrenching memory grew hazy and slipped away.

The pain was far more intense now. It was nearly impossible to think straight or focus on anything else.

If you insist on staying, **the voice inside my head murmured,** *stick to the past. It will help dull the pain.*

Alright.

The second I agreed to it, the hospital room disappeared and the past reclaimed me...

...I was too stunned to process what Collin's boss had told me at first. *It just couldn't be true.* How could I live with the fact that the man I'd loved for years had overdosed all alone in the apartment the two of us had shared? *If I had stayed*—if I had been there when it happened—I could have called for help and *he might still be alive.*

Judy had no trouble accepting the truth that I couldn't bear. She told me to go home to my apartment and insisted that I take a week off to grieve before coming back to work.

When I asked her how I was supposed to pay the rent if I missed a week of work, she said I didn't need to worry about that because there would be no charge for the month.

Numb and disoriented, I stood motionless in the center of the kitchen while she loaded my arms up with bags of take-home containers full of food from the diner. I agreed to call if I needed anything. Then I set out for home, wandering down the street toward my apartment building in a daze as a dull ache settled in the pit of my stomach.

Barely aware of how I'd gotten there, I stepped into my apartment. Then I shut and locked the door and headed straight to the kitchen to toss the food that Judy had given me into the trash. Just the thought of eating turned my stomach. Tears streamed down my cheeks as I dug my phone out of my pocket and pulled up the local newspaper's website. Eyes glued to the screen, I absently wandered out of the kitchen and into the living room.

A massive lump formed in my throat as I dropped into the nearest armchair and scanned through the names on the screen, hoping to God that it was all just some sick twisted joke. Then I found it.

Collin's obituary.

A strangled cry barreled up my throat as the phone slipped from my hand, and I fell apart. Silent gut-wrenching sobs racked my body until I finally exhausted myself enough to drift off to sleep, curled up in an awkward ball in the chair.

There were no comforting visits from angels in my dreams. Instead, I slipped into a deep dreamless slumber, devoid of any hope that anything would ever get better.

I didn't attend Collin's calling hours. I'd never met his family because he wasn't all that close to them and I was afraid that if I met them now, they would blame me for his death...*maybe even as much as I blamed myself.*

Despite my reservations, I couldn't bear the thought of skipping his funeral. I waited until after the service had begun to slip in the back of the church. Then I took a seat near the backdoors, far behind all the other mourners. I kept my head bent, and I wept for the man who had meant the world to me since the day I met him my junior year of college.

As I sat there with my heart crumbling inside my chest, my childhood friend's funeral inevitably came to mind. I squeezed my eyes shut, desperate to feel the warmth of that steady hand on top of mine—like I'd felt at Danny's funeral all those years ago—but I wasn't a naïve child with an overactive imagination anymore. Castiel had been a beautiful childhood fantasy. He had helped me weather the dark storms of my youth and I was grateful for that, but I was an adult now and adults didn't get to be comforted by fictional characters.

How ironic it seemed, to find myself in exactly the same position I'd been in as a stupid child. *What a fool I was to believe that I could find any happiness in this life.*

When the funeral ended, I veered away from the other mourners who were headed downstairs to take comfort in a shared meal. I knew I wouldn't find any comfort there. So, I headed home to grieve alone.

The silence in my apartment was deafening as I fought the overwhelming urge to hit the streets and seek out a dealer who could sell me something that might dull the ache in my heart for a while. Too chicken to search the streets for a dealer and too leery to go to Kurt for a fix, I walked to the liquor store on the corner and spent all the cash I'd been able to find in my apartment. I couldn't bear the thought of spending this solitary week—that Judy had misguidedly sentenced me to—sober, so I drank myself dizzy while I mourned the loss of the love that I'd so selfishly thrown away. I numbed out in front of the television with my old standby, *Supernatural*, until I couldn't keep my eyes open any longer. Then I stumbled off to bed.

I wouldn't admit it to myself, but part of me stupidly hoped that after watching all those hours of *Supernatural*, I might dream of the angel who visited my dreams during the dark days of my childhood. Instead, I slept like the dead and woke with an ache in my heart that was a thousand times worse than the ache in my head.

For a long while, I just laid there on my back staring up at the ceiling because my brain was still swimming in vodka and I just couldn't muster the energy to get out of bed. Besides, what was the point? I had nothing to live for and no one to love me. As I laid there wallowing in my own misery, some foolish part of my inebriated brain thought of my childhood friend. *What would Danny say to me if he was still around?*

Desperate for an answer, I dragged myself out of bed and stumbled through the rooms of my apartment in search of my cell phone. I scoured the compact space for a good twenty minutes before I finally found my phone—hidden beneath a blanket I'd left in a wadded heap on the couch—but when I tried to turn it on, the battery was dead. *Well, didn't that just figure?* A whispered sob escaped my mouth as I set out to hunt for a charger.

By some small miracle, it didn't take long to find a charger lying on the kitchen counter. I attached it to my phone, then plugged the other end into the outlet above the countertop. As the screen came to life, I let out a sigh of gratitude and brought up the playlist my friend had made for me all those years ago. Then I put the music on shuffle so Danny could deliver his message to me from the great beyond.

As soon as Sting's "Why Should I cry for You?" began to play, I set the song on repeat. It wouldn't be right to choose a different song with a happier message, because the question was Danny's to answer, and this was his utterly heartbreaking response. I squeezed my eyes shut as Sting's achingly beautiful melody echoed through my small kitchen. My heart throbbed at the lyrics, and I broke down in tears as my body crumpled to the floor.

For a brief moment in time, I had been a part of something incredible, but I selfishly discarded the love that God had entrusted to me. *It was my fault that Collin was dead.* Another girlfriend—*a better girlfriend*—might have kept him alive.

It broke my heart that I had let Collin down. I'd stopped fighting for him, and now he was gone. *What good was I to anyone?* I was worthless and weak, and my life was a pointless waste. *I was nothing but a pointless waste of space.* I'd failed to protect the only two people who had ever loved me. Danny and Collin were both dead and gone, and I didn't deserve to keep on living in a world without them. I didn't *want* to live in a world without them.

Then a merciful thought occurred to me. *There was a simple enough solution.* I slapped my cheek as hard as I could to stop myself from blubbering like a drunken fool. Then I wiped the tears from my cheeks with my shirtsleeve as I clumsily got to my feet.

I moved toward the medicine cupboard across the kitchen at a slow but determined pace and bit my lip as I pulled the cabinet door beside the refrigerator open. Sting's angelic voice continued to taunt me from the far counter as I took a quick inventory of the drugs I had on hand.

I pulled the over-the-counter medicines out of the cupboard and found a few older prescription bottles tucked away in the back. I always kept them, just in case I ever needed something similar in the future. Most of them weren't helpful at all. There were a few antibiotics that I'd been too wasted to finish like I should have, and a few drugs that I couldn't even recall what they'd been prescribed for. Then I found it, a pill that my doctor had prescribed years ago when I was having trouble falling asleep. I took the bottle out of the cupboard with a trembling hand and fumbled to remove the child safety cap with my impaired dexterity. Most of the pills were still in the bottle. Downing all of them would probably be enough to put an end to this waking nightmare. *It had to be.*

I left the safety cap lying on the counter below the medicine cupboard, and carried the open pill bottle to a nearby cupboard stocked with a meager assortment of mismatched drinking glasses and coffee mugs. I pulled the cupboard door open with a renewed sense of purpose and took out an oversized glass mug. A tear slid down my cheek as I remembered our date at the seafood restaurant where Collin had dutifully drained every drop of that God-awful massive blue cocktail, just so we could take the mug home. In fact, he'd earned a second one by downing the majority of my drink so we could have a matching set. Tears streamed down my cheeks as a hopeless smile spread across my face. *We were so happy back then.* Everything had been perfect, but I'd gone and screwed it all up.

I clutched the mug and the open bottle of pills to my chest as I carried them over to the sink. Then I turned on the faucet, and a moronic thought flitted through my head. I normally filtered the tap water before drinking it. For a split second, I actually considered pouring the tap water down the drain and filling the mug from the pitcher in the fridge with the built-in water filter. *I was such an idiot.* Only I would worry about purifying water to wash down the pills that I was about to poison myself with.

Sting's achingly beautiful tune seemed to swell from the countertop behind me. *Danny was right.* Sting's voice was pure magic, but I didn't deserve the pleasant distraction. I deserved to die in silence, alone and uncomforted. I spun around to stop the music.

And I almost fainted dead away on the spot.

I wasn't dreaming. I knew I was awake, but Castiel—the angel from my childhood dreams—was standing right in front of me, just as real as anyone else. The mug and pill bottle slipped from my hands, sending sleeping pills and shards of broken glass skittering across a puddle of unfiltered tap water at my feet.

"You're..." I blinked back the tears that filled my eyes but more kept coming, blurring the impossible vision standing in front of me. *I wasn't dreaming.* I had just slapped myself across the face a few minutes earlier. That would have woken me up if this was just a dream, *wouldn't it?* "I'm not asleep," I muttered, "This isn't a dream."

"No, it's not," Castiel whispered as his compassionate eyes locked with mine. "You are awake, Abigail."

"Then..." My widened eyes searched the room as if I might find some logical explanation for what I was seeing. "I've lost my mind."

"I know how jarring this must be for you," the angel replied with an apologetic frown, "but I couldn't get through to you, and I couldn't think of any other way to stop you."

I just stood there frozen in place, staring at him with my mouth hanging open for what felt like forever. Finally, I came to my senses enough to shake my head in disbelief. This was ridiculous. *I had to be dreaming.* I struck myself across the face as hard as I could, convinced that a good slap would wake me up. *It had to.*

But my angel still stood there, watching me with those brilliant blue eyes that looked far too ancient to belong to him.

I slapped myself a second time, a little harder than the first. Nothing happened. I didn't wake and he didn't disappear. "This can't be happening," I muttered as I lifted my hand to slap myself a third time.

But he closed the distance between us and grabbed my arm before I could reach my face. "Stop that."

10

"Carry on Wayward Son"

Kansas

The angel's eyes brimmed with disappointment as he released my arm, and my heart sank as its dead weight dropped to my side. He stepped backwards toward the counter behind him without breaking eye contact with me for a second and yet, he somehow managed to avoid every sleeping pill and sliver of broken glass that littered his path.

I watched him in a shell-shocked daze and felt oddly comforted as he tilted his head to one side, to study the playlist on my phone in that familiar not-quite-human Castiel-ish manner. He touched a finger to the screen, silencing Sting's bitter words of hopelessness and lost love. Then he picked the phone up from the counter and scrolled through the list for a few seconds. After making a careful selection with the tip of an index finger, he sat the phone back down on the counter. As "Carry on Wayward Son" began to play, he looked up with a nod of satisfaction.

Despite my utter despair and absolute certainty that I'd lost my mind, a burst of laughter sprang from my mouth at the ridiculousness of it all. "Really?"

The angel studied me through narrowed eyes as he stepped toward me. "Why are you laughing?" He seemed genuinely confused and if I didn't know better, I might also say he looked a bit hurt by my laughter.

In retrospect, I suppose laughing at the celestial being who had just broken the angelic code of conduct to save my life was pretty rude, but at the time I was sure this was all just part of my mental breakdown. "Do you really think that's how we humans work?" I muttered, "Switch the song to the Winchester family anthem and I'll just stop crying, and everything will be all better? You can't just select the song that you think will cheer me up."

He closed the gap between us, avoiding every scrap of the mess on my floor again without ever glancing down. "Why not?"

"You're supposed to put the playlist on shuffle," I muttered like a madwoman, "so Danny can choose the song…" A lump formed in my throat as my voice trailed off. *That sounded insane when I said it out loud.*

The angel tilted his head as he studied me at close range, nearer than any human ever would. "Danny is no longer here, Abigail."

He was just stating the obvious, but his words stung as deeply as if he'd stabbed me with one of the shards of glass at my feet.

"A random selection is just that," he murmured in a regretful tone, "random. There is no message to be gained from shuffling the songs. Choosing one that fits the situation is far more logical."

"Then you should choose one about a mental breakdown."

"I told you," he whispered as his eyes locked with mine, "You are not having a breakdown."

"Right," I muttered, laughing like a lunatic as a tear slid down my cheek, "because if the hallucination standing in your kitchen tells you that you're not crazy, it must be true."

He considered my words of hysteria with a perplexed frown for a few seconds before whispering, "Perhaps you ought to lie down and rest for a bit."

My eyes dropped to the soggy sleeping pills scattered amidst the wet glass fragments on my kitchen floor. *Slicing one of those jagged pieces of glass across my wrists would probably do the trick just as well as the pills.* "I was trying to make that happen."

As soon as I made the split-second decision to squat down and grab a shard of glass, I found myself in the figment of my imagination's arms.

Faster than I could blink an eye, the two of us were in my bedroom. Insane and impossible as this entire scenario was, a rush of panic gripped me as he sat me down on the bed. Figment of my imagination or not, he was here and he cared about me. That was a hell of a lot more than I had going for me in reality. The last thing I wanted to do was close my eyes to get some sleep, only to wake and find myself alone again.

A reassuring smile spread across his face as he met my eyes. "I am not going anywhere," he whispered, as if sensing my panic, "but you need to rest."

"If I close my eyes," I muttered, no longer certain of anything, "I'm afraid I'll wake up and find that this was all just a dream."

"You are awake," he assured me with a compassionate frown, "but you do require sleep. I promise you, I will still be here when you wake."

My throat was painfully dry, but I managed to choke my response out in a hoarse whisper, "How can I know that for sure?"

He exhaled a regretful sigh as he took a step back from my bed. "You will just have to trust me, Abigail."

"Where are you going?" I muttered in an unsteady voice.

He walked across the room and sat down in an armchair against the wall. "I will be right here."

Desperate to keep the conversation going and stall the inevitable, I muttered, "I thought you didn't need to sit."

"I don't," he agreed in a hushed tone that seemed intent on lulling me to sleep, "but you seem more comfortable when I am seated, rather than standing watch over you."

"I…" *He was right.* Having somebody standing in your room, watching over you while you slept, was just plain creepy.

"Creepy?" he whispered as a bemused grin spread across his face, "Is that what I am?"

Too exhausted to continue the discussion, I shook my head. "Could you maybe sit a little closer… please?"

"Of course." His half-grin widened into a compassionate smile as he stood up and carried the bulky armchair across the room to my bedside as if it weighed nothing at all.

Despite my hopelessness, I couldn't help smiling at the angel as he sat back down. "Please stay."

"I told you," he whispered, "I intend to."

Too weary and inebriated to fight sleep off any longer, I let my head drop to the pillow.

As my eyes drooped shut, he drew the blankets up over me. Grateful to have him there, I extended a hand over the side of my bed but instantly regretted the pathetic neediness of the gesture. It was stupid to expect an angel to hold my hand and comfort me like a parent would a frightened child. Not that I'd ever had a parent who would do such a thing, but I'd *read* about parents like that.

I was groggily considering retracting my hand when the world slipped away, and a comforting warmth enveloped me as his hand took hold of mine...

...Engrossed in the memory as I was, it was incredibly disorienting to drift off to sleep in the past, only to brush the surface of consciousness in the present.

It was becoming increasingly difficult to decipher which state was real and which was the dream.

Don't, the voice in my head cautioned. Don't breach the surface here. Stick to the past.

Lost and confused, I allowed the voice to tug me back in time because that was where I longed to be...

11

"Angel"

Dave Matthews Band

Comforted by the presence of the angel beside me, I sunk into an unparalleled state of blissful slumber and I woke with a faint smile on my lips. But as the veil of sleep lifted, I realized I no longer felt the warmth of his hand holding onto mine. Panicked, I opened my eyes.

My heart sank at the sight of the empty chair across the room, exactly where it'd always been. *I was such an idiot.* This was reality. There was no angel watching over me. No matter how desperately I wanted him to be real, Castiel was just a fictional character, and I was one public outburst away from a straitjacket. I tried to recall the details of the previous day but the memories were fuzzy and jumbled, thanks to all the alcohol I'd downed in a sorry attempt to dull the pain.

When exactly had my delusional mind parted from reality? Was it when I was filling the mug with water to down the sleeping pills I found in the cupboard? Maybe some dormant part of me was too afraid to go through with it, and the hallucination was my brain's way of giving me an out from my spur of the moment death-by-pills plan. Or maybe I'd never actually found any pills in my kitchen. *Could the whole thing have been nothing more than an incredibly vivid dream?* There was an easy enough way to figure that much out. If the floor of my kitchen was covered in glass fragments and sleeping pills, then *that* was obviously the pivotal moment when reality and I had parted ways. But *if there was no mess* in the kitchen, I could safely conclude that the whole thing had been nothing more than a grand delusion triggered by an ungodly combination of liquor and grief.

Anxious to scope out the scene in my kitchen, I sat up and tossed the covers off my legs. But as I swung my legs over the side of the bed, the aftereffects of a solid day of drinking brought me to a screeching halt. I didn't have the stomach to deal with that mess just yet. Besides, there was really no rush. I had no place to go for the rest of the week. What harm would there be in taking a long hot shower before tackling the mess in my kitchen, *or the lack thereof?*

I winced at the ache in my head as I stood from the bed and blindly reached for my phone on the bedside table where I normally kept it at night. Then I realized I'd left it lying on the kitchen counter, just as the tips of my fingers connected with it. *What the hell?*

I was sure I'd been listening to Danny's playlist while I was toying with the idea of ending my sorry life with the sleeping pills. *So, how exactly did my phone find its way into the bedroom?* Maybe I'd blacked out for a bit? That could happen when you were stupid drunk. It had happened to Collin on more than one occasion and honestly, that was *the least* of the mysteries from the night before. I'd most likely stumbled to bed with my phone in hand at some point during my blackout, probably right around the same time I started hallucinating.

As I brought Danny's playlist up on my phone, a foggy memory—*of my fictional angel telling me how ridiculous it was to think leaving the song choice up to chance meant anything*—came rushing back to me. Imaginary Castiel was right. Danny was dead and gone. There was nobody who gave a rat's ass about me now, no friend sending me cryptic messages from the great beyond, so the song choice was entirely up to me.

Alright then, what song fit my current situation? A deranged smile spread across my face as "Angel" by the Dave Matthews Band caught my eye. The song seemed like a fitting choice, so I started it playing on repeat and cranked it up nice and loud. Then I headed into the bathroom for a much-needed shower.

I stayed in the shower for a good long while, singing along to my personally selected theme song for the day. Castiel had assured me that there was no logic to a random selection. So, today I would drink myself numb to a song that was both a tribute to my fictional guardian and a mockery to my moronic self for believing in him. Then maybe after I got good and drunk, I might succeed in a fresh attempt to end it all as the song mocked me on repeat.

I sang along to the song with a boisterous enthusiasm that I didn't feel as I stepped out of the shower, toweled myself dry and headed back into my bedroom to slip into fresh clothes.

My stomach growled as I finished getting dressed, angrily reminding me that I hadn't eaten solid food in far too long. Drinking all my meals could only continue for so long; but if I choked down some food, I'd be able to suck down more alcohol before my stomach revolted.

I opened my bedroom door with my phone in hand, still playing my song of the day on repeat, and I sang along at the top of my lungs as I moved down the hall at a snail's pace. But the closer I got to the kitchen, the harder it was to convince myself that I wasn't worried about what awaited me there. I held my breath as I took the final steps toward the kitchen, wondering just how far from sanity I'd stumbled the night before.

My stomach dropped as I reached the doorway and realized I must've lost it big time. I could *smell* a breakfast that I sure as heck didn't remember cooking. Was I stroking out, or had I ingested those pills after all? Maybe this was all part of some elaborate drug-induced dream-state that I had to pass through before my life ended, or maybe my life already *had ended* and this was my own personal hell. That would be just my luck, to end it all only to find that my eternal punishment was a never-ending day in this hellish world—alone and unloved for all eternity—with my sanity crumbling.

I shook those nauseating thoughts from my head as I took that final step and entered the kitchen.

The mess on the floor was gone, *if it had ever actually been there at all.* Had I cleaned it up at some point during my blackout? Or maybe none of that had ever really happened...or I was dead and gone, and there was no evidence of my failed suicide attempt because I'd succeeded. God help me. *I didn't have a clue.*

That's when my eyes settled on the plate of eggs, bacon and toast that was sitting on the far counter. *What the hell?* I wasn't sure if I even had that stuff in my kitchen. Maybe Judy had slipped in while I was showering and left me something to eat because she knew I'd be taking crappy care of myself. It seemed like a bit of a stretch, but what other logical explanation could there possibly be?

I approached the plate at a hesitant pace, as if it might spring to life and attack me at any moment. *Who the hell knew at this point?* The food looked and smelled real enough, so I probably wasn't hallucinating.

My stomach rumbled, as if to say, *who the hell cares how it got there? Just feed me.*

Baffled and unsure what else to do—or how to even *attempt* to explain any of this—I picked up the fork beside the plate and stabbed a bite of scrambled egg. My stomach growled as I lifted the fork and stuck a tentative bite in my mouth.

It certainly *tasted* real and surprisingly satisfying. I had expected my stomach to turn when I finally fed it something solid, but my stomach gratefully accepted that first bite. So, I picked up the toast and nibbled a bite off the corner. Again, my stomach seemed pleased with the offering, so I picked up a slice of bacon. It was perfectly cooked, crispy but not overly so. I let out a hushed moan as I bit into it. It had been ages since I'd eaten bacon.

Now fairly confident that the food wasn't going to hurt me, I picked up the plate and headed to the living room to finish it. My eyes were on the plate as I stepped in the room.

His deep voice startled me half to death as he inquired, "How is it?"

It was a wonder I didn't drop the plate because I lost all sense of feeling in my limbs as I looked up from the plate and gawked at the angel sitting on my couch. *Words escaped me.*

"I have never prepared food before," Castiel confided with an apologetic frown, "but I mimicked what I've watched you do. I would have tasted it to be sure it was edible, but I don't eat."

"I..." *Nope. Still no words.* What the hell was I supposed to say, *or think?*

The angel's brow furrowed with concern. "I startled you again, didn't I?"

I nodded because I still couldn't remember how to form a coherent sentence.

Sorrow shimmered in his beautiful blue eyes as he smiled at me. "Is the food alright?"

"Yes," I finally managed to mutter, "Thank you." Deciding there was really no other option but to go with it, I moved to the couch and sat down next to him. "Am I still dreaming?"

"No," he whispered, "You're awake."

"So," I glanced down at the plate of food in my hands then back up at him, "this is real?"

"It is," he confirmed with a nod.

I sat the plate down on the coffee table in front of me because I was too numb to deal with it. "How can you...be here?"

I looked up from the coffee table, and his eyes locked with mine as he replied, "I promised you that I wouldn't leave."

"I uh... Thanks," I muttered like an idiot. "Where um...where did you get the food?"

A sheepish grin spread across his angelic face. "Alright, technically I did leave to get the ingredients, but you were sound asleep and it took me less than a minute to gather them and return."

Too overwhelmed to even think to question how on earth he had done that, I muttered, "And the mess on my floor?"

His brow furrowed with concern as he whispered, "I took care of it."

The gentleness of his hushed tone warmed my insides. "Thank you."

"It seemed only fair," he replied with a nod, "considering I was the reason you dropped everything in your hands."

"You were trying to save my life," I muttered.

He tilted his head to one side as he considered my response. "*Trying*?"

A few stray tears slid down my cheeks, but wiping them away just didn't seem worth the effort. "I thought I might give it another go today…"

"Abigail," Castiel chided in a deeper tone, "It is not your time."

"I've had enough time," I answered in a broken whisper, "I don't think I want any more…" There was so much more that I wanted to say to him but as my breath hitched in my throat, the words escaped me.

There was a pained expression on the angel's face as he watched my pitiful display of emotion with his sturdy frame hunched in an awkwardly rigid pose.

Too emotionally weak to bear the disappointment in his eyes, I dropped my head in my hands.

He exhaled a tense breath as I sat there falling apart in front of him like a child. Then he slid closer. Slow and uncertain, he wrapped his arms around me.

Danny's arms had been a haven during my childhood. I felt stronger with my dear friend beside me, and my troubles had always melted away whenever I listened to him telling one of his stories. Years later, Collin's arms became my oasis. My first love's embrace made me feel loved and protected in a way that I had never experienced before. I felt entirely at peace when his arms were around me.

But the arms that held me now were like nothing I'd ever experienced, or even dreamed of. This was different than the warmth that touched my hand the day of Danny's funeral. It was different than all the nights I'd dreamt of the angel's hand resting on top of mine and felt warm and comforted by his presence. This wasn't a dream or a vague sensation. I was awake and he was sitting on the couch beside me. *The feeling of serenity was indescribable.* No bliss could ever be greater than Castiel's embrace. This had to be what heaven felt like.

I melted in the angel's arms as my head dropped to his shoulder and the tension seeped from my body, far more tension than I had any idea I'd been carrying around with me. Constantly bracing for the next blow was something I'd been doing for so long, that I had no idea I was even doing it. But there was no need to brace myself for anything in this celestial creature's arms. I knew without a doubt that no harm would come to me while I was with Castiel.

A lifetime of pent-up tears spilled from my eyes in the safety of his arms, and the heartache that I carried with me at all times slipped away with the tears. Crazy as it sounds, it felt as if he lessened my burden by absorbing all of my pain.

If this was what awaited me in heaven, why would I want to stay on earth?

12

"Nights in White Satin"
The Moody Blues

I'm not sure how long I wept. It felt like forever while I was in his arms; but as soon as my tears died away, he straightened and dropped his arms to his sides. A cold emptiness settled inside me as he released me from that warm embrace, and it seemed as if I'd only been in his arms for a matter of seconds. I sat up a little straighter and stared at the angel sitting beside me on the couch. *This couldn't possibly be real, could it?*

Castiel leaned toward me and brushed the tears from my cheeks with the tips of his fingers, and just that slight touch of warmth was enough to fill me with an all-encompassing sense of peace. For a moment he just sat there and watched me.

I had no idea what to say, or what he might be thinking. Terrified that any action I took might break the spell that was keeping him there with me, I didn't dare speak or move.

He dropped his hand from my cheek with a melancholy smile, and my heart sank as he stood up from the couch. Sensing my worry, he shook his head. "I am not leaving, Abigail." His eyes dropped to the plate of food on the coffee table. "You need to eat."

I nodded, then numbly picked up the plate and sat it on my lap. *I would do anything he asked me to as long as he stayed.* Determined to please him, I stabbed a bite of egg and popped it in my mouth.

As he stepped away from the couch, my heart started racing.

"I will be right back," he whispered as he headed into the kitchen.

Despite his assurance that he wasn't going to leave, I stared at the door with my heart in my throat until he stepped back in the room with my phone in his hand. With each step he took toward the couch, the tension knotting every muscle in my body relaxed a bit more.

He sat back down beside me, then turned his attention to the phone in his hand and stopped "Angel" from playing.

I raised an eyebrow, but didn't ask why he'd stopped the music because my mouth was full of toast. *Had my song choice offended him?*

Without waiting for me to ask the question, he looked up from the phone and smiled at me. "I believe it's my turn to choose a song."

I continued dutifully eating the breakfast the angel had made for me as I watched him scroll through the playlist. It didn't take him long to select "Nights in White Satin" by The Moody Blues.

I swallowed the food in my mouth as he sat the phone down on the coffee table. "Is there a reason why you chose that song?"

His eyes dropped to the phone as he shrugged his shoulders. When he looked back up at me, all of my worries melted away with the warmth of his smile. "I have always been fond of this one."

I opened my mouth, but closed it without commenting as the full implication of his response sunk in. *Always?*

"I am always with you, Abigail," he replied, as if I had asked.

"You…" Heat rushed to my cheeks as I whispered, "What?"

The smile that spread across his angelic face could've melted an arctic winter in a matter of seconds. "I told you years ago, I am your guardian. It is my job to watch over you, always."

Maybe that should've creeped me out, but it didn't. The idea that this compassionate creature was always watching over me relaxed a tight knot of dread that had dwelt in the pit of my stomach for as long as I could remember. "That was just a dream."

"It was," he agreed, "but my visits to you were no less real."

"But…" I dropped my eyes to the plate on my lap because the intensity of his stare seemed like too much to bear without bursting into flames. I might as well have been staring straight into the sun. "This is *different*."

"It is," he murmured, "You aren't dreaming this time."

I looked back up at him, desperate to feel the warmth that radiated from him, even if it cost me my vision. "This doesn't make any sense."

"I also explained that years ago," Castiel whispered, bathing me in the warmth of his radiant smile. "You believed in me as a child because human children trust without limits, but adulthood is different. The idea that an angel watches over you, day and night, is too frightening a concept for an adult to accept."

"Frightening?" I muttered, dropping my gaze to the plate to give my eyes a break from his light. "I've never felt safer in my life."

As I lifted my eyes to meet his, the angel's brow furrowed. "This was never meant to happen."

My heart physically ached at his words. "*What* was never meant to happen?"

Regret replaced the joy that'd illuminated Castiel's eyes a moment earlier. "We angels are not meant to reveal ourselves to humans."

"Then…" I concentrated on keeping my voice even as I muttered, "Why did you show yourself to me?"

"I could not allow you to cut your life short," he replied with an apologetic frown.

My throat constricted as I opened my mouth to speak, but I forced my question out in a strangled burst of syllables, "Why does it sound like you regret stopping me?"

"I do not regret stopping you, Abigail," he replied in a hoarse whisper. "If I had the choice to make over again a thousand times, I would stop you every single time."

I could almost feel his earnest tone and compassionate smile mending old hurts buried deep inside me. "So...why was it never meant to happen?"

He dropped his eyes to the coffee table as he shook his head. "It just is not done."

"Why not?" A conversation that we'd had in a dream years earlier came rushing back to me, with a clarity that rarely accompanies memories of dreams, and my heart ached for the angel sitting beside me. *Why would God condemn his angels to such a lonely existence?*

"There are rules," he replied in a hushed tone.

I wanted to ask him to explain what that meant, but I didn't want to get him into any more trouble than I already had. He'd already broken the angelic rules of conduct for me. The thought of this miraculous being disobeying a command from heaven *for me* was incomprehensible. Helping a worthless creature like me couldn't possibly be worth risking whatever consequences would come from breaking the Lord's rules.

"You are wrong," he murmured, once again answering my unspoken thought. "*You truly are precious*, Abigail. I am so sorry that you don't believe that to be true."

Tears filled my eyes, but I couldn't find words to respond.

"I feel as though I have failed you," he whispered, "allowing so much hurt to come to you and warp your opinion of your own worth."

I shook my head and muttered, "I'm not worth much."

Tears swam in the angel's eyes as he whispered, "You are just proving my point."

It pained me to see so much sorrow in those beautiful eyes. I would have done anything to take that hurt away.

"I have been beside you for every emotional trauma," he whispered, "I know how much pain this life has dealt you, and I wish I could have prevented all of it. But that is not the way of things. We angels are meant to watch over and guide the soul we are responsible for, but we are not to alter the course of life events—"

"But you stopped me last night," I muttered, lost in the depths of those ancient blue eyes. I was sure I could drown in those perfect pools of blue if I focused on them for too long.

"Yes, I've broken more than a few rules with you," he whispered, "I couldn't stand by and watch you take your own life. Trust me, Abigail. You would not have ended up where you were hoping to go."

What did that mean? *Was I already destined for hell, or would killing myself have bought me a one-way ticket downstairs?*

"I cannot answer those questions." Something in those tortured angelic eyes pleaded with me to let it drop. He said he had already *broken more than a few rules* for me. Was it possible that he *would* give me the answers that he wasn't supposed to share, if I asked him to?

I was tempted to press him for answers, but unwilling to add to the hurt in his eyes. *Nothing* was worth causing my angel more pain. No matter how badly I wanted to know what awaited me in the afterlife, I couldn't ask him. "I can't take any more of this."

He exhaled a tense breath. "I am afraid you don't have a choice."

I looked back up at him. "Are you saying that you would stop me if I tried to end my life again?"

"A thousand times," he replied in a hoarse rasp, "Weren't you listening to me earlier? I assure you, I meant that quite literally."

The thought of being trapped in this God-awful existence until I shriveled up and turned gray was too suffocating to accept. "Then I'll just have to try a thousand and one times."

"Abigail," he practically growled.

"I can't live with it," I whimpered.

"With what?" he asked in a much softer tone.

"You know my thoughts," I muttered, my voice little more than a choked whisper, "So, you must know what I'm talking about. It's *my fault* that Collin is dead."

"No, it is not." Castiel appeared to be in almost as much pain as I was as he whispered, "Collin made his own choices. The fault was his."

I tilted my head back to stare up at the ceiling, as if God were up there watching us. "If I had stayed with him…"

Castiel reached out and took hold of my hand as he whispered, "You would have ended up like him."

"Maybe that would've been for the best," I sobbed, afraid to take my eyes off the ceiling because I couldn't stand the look of disapproval in his eyes.

"Your life is precious," he replied, squeezing my hand to emphasize his words, "Sacrificing it, because someone you loved was stuck in a self-destructive pattern of behavior, would have been an unforgivable offense."

Despite my reluctance to look him in the eye, I couldn't help dropping my gaze to his. "An offense to *who?*"

"To the Lord," Castiel whispered, "and to me."

"You don't understand," I sobbed in a broken whisper, "The guilt that I feel...knowing that I walked away from him instead of staying to help him...to talk him into turning his life around... You don't know how much that hurts."

His angelic eyes darkened, and the silence stretched out between us as the last words I'd spoken hung in the void.

Something about this silence felt too heavy. It seemed to weigh down the air, making it harder to breathe. I wanted to ask him what he was thinking or what I could do to help. *But what comfort could I possibly offer him?* I was just a weak broken human. He wasn't supposed to share his thoughts with me—or even show himself to me, for that matter.

In their darkened state, his eyes appeared far older than ancient. I know that sounds like nonsense, but I glimpsed something timeless in those darkened depths of blue—something that I doubt any human was ever meant to witness.

He cleared his throat and dropped his eyes to my hand, as if sensing that he'd allowed me to see too much. "I think it's time for me to tell you my story, Abigail."

13

"Wicked Game"

Chris Isaak

Castiel must not have put "Nights In White Satin" on repeat when he started it playing because just as he suggested that it was time for him to share his story, the song ended. The silence that followed seemed to swallow up every last bit of the world but the couch that the two of us were sitting on. My entire apartment building could have gone up in flames and I doubt I would've even noticed. I wanted to hear my angel's story, *more than I'd ever wanted anything*. Something in his eyes told me that he had carried this pain that he no longer seemed able to hide *forever*.

Focused as I was on Castiel, I almost jumped out of my skin when Chris Isaak's "Wicked Game" shattered the weighted silence between us. Even if I'd wanted to get up and change the song, I don't think I could have moved.

My angel didn't even seem to notice the music. The far-off look in his eyes told me that he'd already drifted back to the past—the ancient past—where his story began. "Your modern Bible does not tell the entire story," Castiel confided in a gravely whisper, as if his hushed tone could prevent the Lord from hearing. "When the organized religions of this world were just beginning to form, the earliest leaders of the church chose to omit the sections of the Bible that did not mesh with their version of the story. Those sacred texts are now referred to as the lost books of the Bible, and my story lies within the pages of one of them—The Book of Enoch—forgotten by most of the inhabitants of the modern world."

Chris Isaak's voice had given me goose bumps since the day I'd first listened to "Wicked Game" on Danny's playlist. The fact that this song just happened to be the randomly selected background music to Castiel's story gave it an eerie quality that chilled me to the bone, but I didn't dare stop the music. I didn't want to risk doing anything that might break the angel's concentration and make him change his mind about sharing his story with me.

Castiel noticed my slight shiver and placed his hand on top of mine, chasing away the cold with the serenity of his warmth. "After He created this world, the Lord chose a select group of angels to remain here on earth. I was one of those angels. We were called the Watchers because we were intended to remain in our spiritual state and watch over God's creations, unseen by the eyes of men. For a time, that is exactly what we all did. But as man began to procreate and populate the earth, many of the Watchers took notice of the beauty of the daughters of men. They thought it was unfair that men should be allowed to lie with those fair creatures while we celestial beings remained hidden in the shadows, serving no purpose but to watch over the actions of men. Eventually—when the majority of the Watchers were of that same opinion—our leader, Semjaza, suggested that we all make a pact. It was a plan born out of cowardice. Semjaza feared that if he gave in to temptation and the rest of us did not follow, then he alone would have to bear the punishment for this grievous sin. Semjaza reasoned that if we all took human wives, the blame would be shared amongst the lot of us and the punishment would be less severe. The Book of Enoch states that all two-hundred Watchers who had been assigned to earth agreed to this pact and chose wives from among the daughters of men, but Enoch's account of the story was not entirely accurate. There were actually three-hundred Watchers on earth in those days. The two-hundred who followed Semjaza descended into the physical realm on the Summit of Mount Hermon where they all swore an oath, binding themselves by mutual curses so that none of them could go back on the plan. However, the other one-hundred of us refused to break the Lord's rules by defiling ourselves in that way."

Defiling ourselves? Castiel was so engrossed in the telling of his story that I don't think he noticed the way I flinched at his choice of words. *Were we humans just filthy lesser creatures to him?* It only took me a few seconds to realize that I was being an idiot. This angel was sitting on my couch confiding in *me*, the human he had broken multiple rules for. It was ridiculous to be offended by a comment that he'd made about angels cross-pollenating with humans at the beginning of time.

"Those of us who refused to take the oath—and bind ourselves with Semjaza and his followers— dispersed from the others and fled, and we continued to watch." Castiel's eyes grew a shade darker as he whispered, "We watched…while Semjaza and the others took human wives and impregnated them…and we remained hidden while they gave birth to the Nephalim—a race of Giants—who were the unholy offspring of human and angel. Semjaza and the rest of the fallen Watchers settled into a peaceable existence among the humans. They taught them how to craft weapons, how to adorn themselves with jewels and paint their faces, they taught spells and counter-spells, and root-cutting and astrology. They shared their knowledge of the sun, the moon, and the clouds and taught men how to interpret the signs of the earth—and all of that knowledge corrupted the hearts of men and led them astray— and man turned away from God."

Castiel's attention shifted back to the present. His brow furrowed and his head tilted as he searched my eyes for a reaction to what he had just shared with me.

It took a conscious effort for me to tear myself out of immobility but I managed a slight nod, urging him to go on with his story because I needed to hear the rest of it.

"As the children of men grew corrupt in their ways, the children of the Watchers grew up. The adult Nephalim devoured the fruits of men's labor and when men could no longer provide enough to sustain this insatiable horde of Giants, they turned on the human race. The Nephalim spread out and roamed the earth, killing and defiling—one another, the sons of man and every living creature of God's creation— in unspeakable ways..." Castiel's voice trailed off as his focus shifted back to me, and the haunted look in his darkened eyes broke my heart.

Almost as engrossed in the telling of his tale as he was, it took me a few seconds to find my voice and whisper, "Tell me more."

"Those of us who fled..." Castiel squeezed his eyes shut as he muttered, "We should have stayed and tried harder to stop our brothers from ever making that pact. Perhaps if we had, we could have prevented all the lawlessness and bloodshed that resulted from their actions."

I shook my head and whispered, "You can't possibly blame yourself for all of *that*."

"No?" Castiel opened his eyes and smiled at me, but it was a tortured smile. "Is it so different from you blaming yourself for failing to stop Collin's self-destruction?"

The air in my lungs escaped me in an agonized rush at the mention of Collin. *Was it any different?* "I failed to help my boyfriend," I muttered, "You can't compare failing to stop a pack of immortal creatures—who outnumbered you two to one—from destroying the earth, with me failing to stay and support the only man who ever loved me."

"You said that I could not understand your guilt over leaving to protect yourself, rather than staying to prevent the destruction of another," he replied in a rough whisper, "I am telling you that I *do* understand, Abigail."

"I'm so sorry," I muttered, "I had no idea…"

We sat there in silence for a few minutes, both of us lost in our own thoughts.

But I wanted to hear the rest of his story. "So, what happened?" I muttered, "I mean, why aren't there still Giants running around destroying everything in our world today?"

Castiel's brow furrowed, as if he were trying to decide whether or not to share more than he already had. Then he cleared his throat and answered, "God wiped the slate clean."

The absoluteness of that statement made my mouth go dry. "How?"

"He flooded the earth," my angel replied as his ancient eyes locked with mine, "destroying all but a righteous man and the handful of humans and creatures he was instructed to bring into the Ark with him."

My mouth had gone so dry that just the thought of trying to talk hurt my throat. I swallowed in an attempt to provide some moisture, but it didn't help at all. "Noah's Ark?" I croaked.

Castiel's eyes remained locked with mine as he nodded.

"But you survived," I whispered in a hoarse rasp.

Sorrow darkened my angel's eyes a bit more as he replied, "All of the Watchers survived, but not without consequence."

A chill crept down my spine as I whispered, "What consequence?"

"Azazel, the Watcher who taught men how to forge weapons, was blamed for the corruption of the entire earth and for all sins that followed. For this grievous infraction, the Lord instructed the archangel Raphael to bind Azazel hand and foot, split open the earth in the desert of Dudael and cast him into the darkness. Raphael did as the Lord commanded. Then he filled the hole in with jagged rocks and left Azazel to remain there in the darkness until the end of days when he is to be hurled into the fire." Castiel drew a ragged breath then focused upward as he blinked back the tears in his eyes. "The archangel Gabriel was instructed to destroy the children of the Watchers. At the Lord's command, he twisted the minds of the Nephalim, causing them to turn against one another until the entire lot of them were destroyed in battle. After Semjaza and the other fallen Watchers had witnessed the destruction of everything that they held dear, God sent Michael to bind them all and bury them deep beneath the hills of the earth until judgment day, when they are to be tossed into the abyss and burned along with the rest of the condemned."

Tears streamed down my cheeks for Castiel's fallen brothers. *All of that wrath, just for falling in love?* "What about you and the other Watchers who fled," I whispered, "what happened to you?"

"When Semjaza and the others first acted on their decision to fornicate with human women, they rendered themselves unable to return to their purely spiritual state. They became trapped in the physical realm and the gates of heaven were sealed shut, so the rest of us were also incapable of returning home. Once we were cut off from heaven, we no longer received direction from the Lord or our fellow angels. Many of the remaining one-hundred chose to take physical form and find wives of their own because they didn't know what else to do."

"What did you do?" I asked in a feeble whisper.

"I continued doing what I had been placed on earth to do. *I watched.* For centuries," Castiel muttered as his darkened eyes met mine, "I stayed...and I watched."

But I still couldn't connect all the dots. There had to be more to this story. "So...how the heck did you end up getting stuck with *me?*"

Castiel's eyes were ripe with disappointment as he frowned at me. "I did not *get stuck* with you, Abigail. I was given a second chance to fulfill my purpose."

I shook my head and lowered my eyes to the couch as I muttered, "How could watching *me* fulfill your purpose?"

"After I was, for all intents and purposes, left behind and locked out of heaven," he whispered, "I spent ages attempting to do penance for my mistakes."

Mistakes? I still didn't get it. Castiel never agreed to the Watchers' pact. *He didn't do anything wrong.* I looked up and searched his eyes as I whispered, "What mistakes?"

"I fled, Abigail," he replied with a sorrowful smile, "I may not have chosen to join Semjaza and the others, but I also did not return to heaven to report what they planned to do because I couldn't bring myself to have a hand in my brothers' punishment. My *indecision* was my sin. I failed to take a side, and I stayed silent while all those grievous misdeeds were done."

"Guilt by default," I muttered, "that doesn't seem very fair. So, how exactly did you try to do penance for your mistakes?"

"After Semjaza and the others were buried beneath the earth, the Watchers who remained were scattered. I was entirely on my own and without direction," Castiel whispered, "so I vowed to do all that I could to guide men in the right direction in order to atone for my mistakes. I sought out the war-torn regions of this world throughout the ages, and I did everything within my power to change the hearts of those involved. Since I had no specific orders to follow, I made it my own personal mission to change the hearts of the leaders and the followers of war, and I sought to convert the hearts of as many wrong-doers as possible. I figured that if I could right enough wrongs and do enough good, then my choice to flee would be forgiven. For thousands of years, I worked to effect changes for good on a global scale because I was certain that eventually the Lord would notice all that I had accomplished."

I nodded and whispered, "Did you, uh…make things better on a global scale, like you wanted to?"

"Yes, I did," he replied with a wistful smile, "I brought about major changes, but my overall contribution to the Lord's plan was miniscule."

I still didn't get it. "Why?"

"Why?" he echoed in a rough whisper. "That was the question that haunted me through the ages. Why weren't all of my efforts enough? What more could the Lord possibly want from me?"

I drew a tense breath and whispered, "And…did you ever figure that out?"

A smile lit up Castiel's angelic face as he wiped a tear from my cheek with the tip of his index finger. His eyes were less dark and tortured than they were when he'd started telling his tale. "Not until quite recently," he whispered, "not until you."

I swallowed, and blinked at him a few times before muttering, "Me?"

"Yes," he replied as he touched a hand to my cheek. "When Gabriel first came to me—to inform me that the Lord was assigning me to guard a single soul that was about to enter the world—I was confused and quite frankly, I was angry. After all of my global accomplishments, I could not understand why the Lord would demote me to babysitting a single soul."

"Sorry," I muttered.

"Don't be," he whispered as he took his hand from my cheek and placed it on top of my hand, "I was wrong."

I looked down at our hands as his warmth seeped into me. "You were wrong about *what*?"

"I was misguided," he muttered, "I had been for ages. It took the honor of becoming your guardian for me to finally grasp what had never occurred to me in all those years."

I felt my cheeks blush as I whispered, "And what's that?"

"I didn't understand that guarding one precious soul was a far more important task than watching over a multitude of humans."

I looked up at his face and my cheeks flamed when I saw the way he was smiling at me, as if I were something special. "It is?"

"Yes," he whispered, "It took *you* to teach me that grand gestures are, for the most part, empty gestures."

"How could doing all that good be an empty gesture?"

"Grand gestures do not require true compassion," he whispered, "I had always sought to accomplish magnificent deeds of grand importance. I aimed to change the hearts of all men because I failed to understand that it is *impossible* for one being to be something to everyone. Watching over you helped me to realize that, while it is not possible to be something to everyone, *it is possible to be everything to someone.*"

Now *that* I understood. Castiel *was* everything to me. I couldn't begin to imagine how much worse my life would've been if Castiel hadn't been beside me, visiting my dreams and watching out for me through all of it. Tears filled my eyes as I muttered, "I don't know what to say."

"Promise me that you will not give up," he whispered, "Just live, Abigail. Instead of attempting to end your life, use the life that God gave you to make this world a better place. Look for every small opportunity to make a difference in someone else's life. Those quiet uncelebrated acts of kindness with no expectation of personal gain, those are the actions that truly matter in the end."

"I promise," I whispered as I swiped at the tears on my cheeks with the sleeve of my shirt, "but what will happen to *you* after I die?"

He grinned at me. It was a melancholy grin but his eyes were nothing short of radiant. "I will get to go home."

"So...I'm your ticket back to heaven?" *How could I possibly end my life?* If Castiel's salvation was in my hands, I vowed right then and there to do whatever it took to get him home.

His melancholy grin widened. "That is not how I look at it."

"How else *could* you look at it?" I muttered.

"Guiding you is its own reward, Abigail. If I were doing this to help myself, I would still be missing the point."

"What point?"

"The most important task that I have ever undertaken, is the task of guiding you to your eternal resting place," he whispered, "This is not about *me*. It is about guarding your precious soul as you walk the path of life, and guiding you to remain on the right path so that you will be welcomed into heaven with open arms."

I nodded because I couldn't seem to find my voice. It felt as if a switch had been flipped inside me. For Castiel, this might not be about him but from now on, it *was* going to be about him for me. I was going to devote the rest of my life to doing good, so that he could return to heaven. *How could I not?* After all, he'd said it himself. *He was everything to me.*

14

"Blue Eyes Crying In the Rain"
Willie Nelson

Almost as if on cue, "Wicked Games" stopped playing as the two of us fell silent. After a pregnant pause, Willie Nelson's "Blue Eyes Crying In the Rain" began to play. A knowing smile spread across Castiel's face, and I couldn't help wondering if he knew that the song had played during an episode of *Supernatural* while Castiel said goodbye to Claire Novak and watched her taxi drive away. No matter how many times I watched that episode, the look on the angel's face at the end of that scene never failed to make me tear up.

The darkness that'd filled Castiel's eyes while he was sharing his story with me was gone now. Once again, his eyes were a radiant source of light that practically blinded me. Although, I could still detect a hint of that timeless agony. Now that I knew the angel's story, I suspected I might always be able to see it. *Always...*

As I sat there staring into those bottomless depths of blue, it occurred to me that there probably wouldn't be an *always* for the two of us. Before Castiel shared his story, I'd been terrified that every second with him could be the last second before he disappeared and returned to the spiritual plane. The thought of him leaving me after all of this was unbearable. *How was I supposed to go on without him?*

My angel's eyes mirrored my pain as he whispered, "I've just shared everything that I have to share with you, Abigail. Now it's your turn. Tell me what's troubling you."

I drew a ragged breath and whispered, "I don't get to keep you here with me, do I?"

Every feature of Castiel's angelic face—his furrowed brow, the tears glistening in his brilliant blue eyes, the downward curve of his mouth—all of it was etched in sorrow as he lifted his hand and cupped the side of my face in his palm. "I'm afraid not," he murmured, "at least, not permanently."

I tilted my head toward his hand, leaning into his warmth as I muttered, "How long can you stay here with me?"

He exhaled a reluctant sigh as his thumb stroked my cheek. "Technically, I shouldn't be here in this physical form at all. So, there are no rules for me to follow now that I've crossed this line."

His hand was still cupping the side of my face. Determined to keep it there for as long as I could—to keep *him* with me for as long as I could—I reached up and covered as much of his hand as I could with my smaller palm. "Then will you at least stay a little longer...please?"

The warmth of his smile conveyed a staggering amount of affection, but his eyes still shimmered with regret. He closed his eyes for a moment and when they reopened, he tipped his head forward and touched his forehead to mine.

"Is this a *yes*," I croaked, "or a *goodbye*?"

At this intimate distance with the tops of our heads touching and his hand against my cheek, the intensity of this angel's stare took my breath away. "*This* is my attempt to capture the moment and keep it with me," he murmured, "so that when I return to my spiritual form, I can recall what it felt like to touch you."

A muffled sob escaped my mouth as a tear slid down my cheek.

He drew a deep breath and slowly exhaled, bathing me in his warmth as he brushed the tear from my cheek with his thumb. "I will always be with you, Abigail. Although I understand that human adults cannot accept such a fact, I pray that somehow—after all of this—you will not doubt that it was real when you can no longer see me."

Panic gripped me at the thought of losing him and my heart began to hammer in my chest. "Please…" I lifted my other hand and wrapped it around his wrist, as if my feeble hold could keep him there with me. "Please don't leave me."

"Abigail," he replied in a tortured rasp, "I cannot stay here like this."

"I know," I whimpered, tightening my pathetic hold on his wrist despite my words. "Just…please don't go tonight."

"The longer I remain here like this," he whispered, "the harder I fear it will be to leave you."

"I can't be alone tonight," I sobbed. "Please stay… at least until tomorrow."

He pressed his forehead a bit tighter against mine, closing an undetectable gap between us. "Your employer has granted you three more days of leave. I am not sure that this is the correct thing to do," he whispered as his eyes searched mine, "but I will stay until you return to work, so that you won't feel quite so isolated."

I nodded, then dropped my head to his shoulder and broke down in tears.

This time, his arms wrapped around me without hesitation. It felt like the most natural thing in the world to be tucked against his chest like this, safe within the warmth of his angelic embrace. While I was sobbing in his arms, I almost could've sworn that I heard his breath hitch.

I finally managed to quell my tears by reminding myself that there would be plenty of time for crying after my angel was gone. *We had three days together.* I didn't want to spend another second of what little time we had, sobbing like a child. Castiel said he wanted to memorize the feel of me, so he could recall it after he returned to his spiritual form. I had three days to share as many human experiences as I could with him before he left. A part of me wanted to stay exactly as we were because I didn't ever want to leave the comfort of his arms, but our time was limited and I couldn't afford to waste a second of it.

I lifted my head from his shoulder and sat up a little straighter as I cleared my throat and muttered, "Can you leave this apartment, or do we have to stay here while you're in this form?"

"You can come and go as you like," he whispered, "but I can't leave the apartment in this physical form."

"Then we'll both stay," I muttered, "I don't want to waste a second of our three days."

"I won't actually be leaving you in three days," he reminded me with a tortured expression that eerily mimicked the look on his television counterpart's face as he watched Claire's taxi drive away. "You just won't be able to see me any longer."

I dropped my eyes to the couch cushions. "How is that any different?"

He reached out, took hold of my chin and lifted it—bringing my eyes back to his—with a gentleness that flooded my insides with warmth. "I hope that you will be able to take comfort in the knowledge that I am still there beside you after I leave this physical form."

"Well, you're here now," I muttered, "So, what would you like to do?"

"I am content just to watch you go about your day," he whispered, "assuming you treat yourself with the kindness that you deserve."

I focused on keeping my tone matter-of-fact as I muttered, "You'll be standing back and watching me for the rest of my life. Isn't there anything that you've always wanted to do?"

He tilted his head to one side as he considered my question. "Not really."

"How can that be true? The other Watchers obviously wanted to experience things in the physical world," I whispered as heat rushed to my cheeks, "There must be *something* that you've always wanted to do."

"I have never seen the point in wishing for things that I cannot have. My brothers' weaknesses were not my own," he replied in a contemplative tone, "I felt no jealousy toward man for experiencing things that I was not permitted to."

"Right," I muttered under my breath, "Why would you want to *defile* yourself by doing anything that we humans do?"

He scrutinized me through narrowed eyes, making it clear that he'd picked up on my bitterness at his choice of words. "Their fornication was a sin, Abigail. The coupling of angel and human produced an abomination that plagued the entire world and ultimately led to its destruction at the hands of the Lord. Why does it sound as if you fault me for not joining my brothers in sin?"

"I don't fault you," I muttered with an apologetic frown, "It just stung a little to hear you talk about it, as if we humans were dirty creatures."

"I did not mean to imply that I felt that way," he murmured. "My entire existence has been dedicated to the protection and guidance of human-kind. I love humans as God loves them. I just never understood how the other Watchers could so callously and selfishly desert their appointed posts. Their lustful actions resulted in the destruction of mankind, the race that we were placed on this earth to protect."

Something between a chuckle and a sob hic-cupped from my throat. "Well...when you put it like that, I feel like a terrible person for being offended."

Castiel gave my hand a gentle squeeze. "Nothing that I say or do should ever make you feel like a terrible person."

"Alright," I muttered as my cheeks bloomed with heat. "If you can't think of anything that you'd like to do during our time together, I'll just have to make plans for us."

"Plans that do not involve leaving your apart-ment?" he muttered with a bemused grin.

I dropped my gaze to our joined hands. "I don't care where we spend the time. As long as I have you here with me, heaven exists within these walls."

"Well," he murmured as he brushed a stray tear from my cheek, "When you put it like that, I can't think of anywhere I would rather be."

15

"Your Song"
Ellie Goulding

The voice in my head had warned me to stick to the past now that the pain had become excruciating, but as much as I loved reliving the past with my angel, Danny and Cassie were in the present. They were the reason I was still hanging on, and I needed to know how they were holding up. So, I pushed my way through the drug-induced fog and the mind-numbing pain, clawing my way toward consciousness to get back to my children.

"You haven't changed a bit," **a familiar voice mused,** *"You are still just as stubborn as you were when we were kids."*

That precious voice fueled the final burst of strength that I needed to pry my eyes open. The room was just as blurry as it was the last time I'd regained consciousness, but I could see the figure standing at the foot of my bed

clear as day now. "Danny?" *I croaked in a feeble whisper.*

"I'm right here, Mom." I felt my son take my hand in his as his chair screeched across the floor to my bedside. Even at such an intimate distance, his features were blurred.

My childhood friend grinned from ear to ear as he stepped up from the foot of my bed and sat down on the side opposite my son. "You named your son Danny?"

"After you," I muttered, "You were right, Danny..." My lips were cracked, my mouth felt like it'd been lined with cotton, and my throat was too raw to finish the sentence out loud.

"I was right about what, Mom?" my son whispered as he leaned over the bed and placed his ear close to my mouth.

My childhood friend smiled at me from the other side of the bed as he took my free hand in his. You don't have to speak, Abbie. I can hear you just fine if you think the words.

Tears streamed down my wrinkled cheeks as I tried to nod, but to no avail. It's so good to see you again.

It's good to see you too. *My old friend spun sideways with the sort of youthful agility that had escaped me decades earlier. Then he scooted back to sit beside me on the bed with his long legs stretched out next to mine. An affectionate smile spread across his face as he touched his head to mine, and I couldn't help noticing that his touch felt warmer and more concrete than my son's.*

How are you here, Danny? **I'm not sure why I even asked, since I was pretty sure I already knew the answer. I was closer to where Danny had come from than I was to the world of the living at this point.**

I wouldn't leave you to face this alone, Abbie. You were there for me when I crossed over, remember?

How could I ever forget? **There was so much more that I wanted to say to him, but the pain was making it nearly impossible to sort out my thoughts.**

Don't fight it, Abbie. We'll have plenty of time to talk soon enough. Go ahead. Drift back to the past and finish your journey. I'll be waiting right here for you when you're ready. I promise.

I tried to nod, but I still couldn't manage even that slight movement. My dear friend gave my hand a reassuring squeeze as my eyes drooped shut, and I drifted back to the past—back to him...

...Ellie Goulding's version of "Your Song" greeted me as I resurfaced in the past. Her hauntingly beautiful voice anchored me to the memory almost instantly, chasing away every trace of the pain I'd just drifted away from.

Castiel and I had spent the rest of the daylight hours on my couch, with Danny's music playing softly in the background while we talked about every subject under the sun. I was feeling a bit punchy now that night had fallen, but it was nothing that a pot of coffee or two couldn't fix. Three short days was all the time I had to spend with my angel and I wasn't about to waste a second of it on frivolous things, like sleep. I suppressed a yawn, sat up a little straighter and twisted sideways, propping my torso against the back of the couch to face Castiel as I listened to his story about the war of 1812.

He paused his story midsentence and tilted his head to one side as he studied me. "You are in need of sleep."

I had to fight to keep my traitorous eyelids from drooping as I whispered, "No. I just need some coffee."

"I have been beside you since the day of your birth, Abigail," he murmured as his brow furrowed, "Do you really think I can't tell when you are tired?"

"I can sleep after you're gone…" I let my voice trail off because it sounded much whinier than I'd meant it to. I closed my eyes, took a deep breath and tried again in a more stoic tone, "I don't want to waste a second of our time together."

"Sleep is not time wasted," he murmured. "It is necessary. Besides, you are forgetting something."

I covered my mouth with a hand to conceal a yawn that I couldn't suppress. "What's that?"

"I can visit your dreams," he replied with a reassuring grin, "There is no need for our time together to be interrupted by sleep."

I let my head droop against the back of the couch because it was beginning to feel too heavy to hold upright. "You can do that in your human form?"

"No," he whispered, tilting his head to mirror my movement, "but I am capable of switching between my physical and spiritual forms easily enough."

"No…" Panic tightened my chest, constricting my airway and squeezing my heart till it ached. "What if you can't get back here when I wake up?"

"I can," he whispered.

I exhaled a tense breath. "But…what if you *don't* come back when I wake?"

He reached up and stroked his fingers over my cheek. "I promised you that I would stay."

"I know," I muttered, "but a part of me is still afraid that none of this is real and if I go to sleep, I might wake up in a reality…without you in it."

He let his palm rest against my cheek, comforting me with its warmth. "Trust me, Abigail."

Sleep enveloped me the instant he touched me. As I sank through its murky depths, I vaguely sensed him lifting me off the couch and carrying me to my bedroom. I wanted to protest, but I'd sunken too far from wakefulness to speak, which left me no choice but to trust him.

As he laid me down on the bed, I shouted a desperate mental plea, *Please don't leave me.*

"I am not going anywhere," he whispered as he took a step toward the chair he'd placed at my bedside the night before.

I managed to lift my eyelids just enough to make out the blurred shape of him as I muttered, "No. Stay here beside me…please?"

Castiel turned to face me and stood there, still as a statue for several heartbeats.

"Please," I pleaded in a groggy whisper, "I won't be able to sleep unless I feel you next to me."

My angel's blurry head nodded as he stepped closer and sat down on the edge of my bed. I expected him to perch there rigidly, like he used to when he visited my childhood dreams. Instead, he swung his legs up onto the bed, slid close to me and sank against the mattress so he was lying on his side with his face close to mine.

The warmth of his breath washed over me like a sedative, nudging me back toward sleep. "Trust me, Abigail. I will be right here when you wake." He touched a hand to my cheek, then swept a few wisps of hair back from my face as sleep dragged me into its depths.

I only felt panicked for a second or two. After that, I opened my eyes and found myself on the bed just as I had been. Confused, I narrowed my eyes at the angel lying next to me.

A grin of amusement tugged at the corners of his mouth. "You are asleep now."

"Huh…" I was about to ask if we had to stay on the bed, but decided not to. *Where on earth would I rather be than lying next to the angel of my dreams?*

Perceptive as always, Castiel murmured, "Would you like to continue our conversation here?"

"Yes," I muttered with a slight nod, "I would."

"I think I've gone on about the wars throughout history for long enough," he whispered, "Frankly, I am amazed my stories didn't bore you to sleep hours ago."

I blinked my eyes a few times to rid myself of a groggy sense of disorientation. "I love listening to stories."

"Yes, of course," he whispered, "Danny used to tell you stories all the time."

"He did," I muttered, "It breaks my heart that he never got the chance to share his talent with the world."

A knowing smile spread across Castiel's face. "His talents are not wasted in heaven."

"I'll take your word for it," I muttered, "because I'm sure you can't tell me more than that."

Regret darkened his eyes as he whispered, "I can't, but you can trust my word. I would never lie to you, Abigail."

The sorrow in his voice broke my heart. "I do trust you. Let's not waste any time on questions that you're not permitted to answer."

"Alright," he whispered, but the regret in his eyes didn't dissipate. "How would you like to spend our time together?"

"I want to share as many human experiences as I can with you," I answered, pausing a moment so that he could voice his opinion on the matter. When he didn't comment, I whispered, "Sharing a meal is a favorite way for us humans to spend time together. I know you don't need to eat or drink, but can you?"

"I can watch you eat," he muttered. "Why would I ingest nutrients that I do not require?"

"Because," I whispered, suppressing a smile, "eating is a pleasurable experience for humans. That's why so many of our social gatherings include a shared meal."

Castiel nodded, but he didn't look convinced.

"You don't need to eat an entire plate of food," I muttered. "Just tell me, if I gave you some food and drink, would you be able to try a taste?"

"I suppose," he muttered, his tone as perplexed as his frown.

"Good." *I just hoped that my angel could taste more than molecules.*

"So," he murmured, "You would like us to share a meal when you wake?"

A victorious smile spread across my face as I nodded.

Castiel's brow furrowed, as if a thought had just occurred to him. "You only ate a small portion of the breakfast that I prepared for you this morning. That wasn't nearly enough food to nourish a human for an entire day."

"I haven't had much of an appetite since I found out about Collin," I admitted in a hoarse whisper.

"Then a shared meal would be a splendid way for us to spend our time when you wake," he agreed with a grin...

...I tried to stay in the past like Danny told me to, but the pain wouldn't allow it.

You don't need to keep doing this, Abbie. Just let go of this world, and I can take you away from all of this pain.

I tried to open my eyes and look at Danny, but I couldn't muster the strength to lift my eyelids. I can't leave until I know Danny and Cassie are ready to say goodbye.

*Dang, you're stubborn, **my childhood friend murmured close to my ear. I could still feel his warm hand holding onto mine.** I know exactly how much pain you're in. Cancer is what took me too. Remember?*

How could I forget?

*Go back to him, **Danny whispered in my ear.***

He gave me a gentle shove, and I drifted back to the past as if we were floating in water...

16

"You and Me"
Lifehouse

Castiel and I were sitting on a blanket on the rooftop of my apartment building. The sun was just beginning to sink toward the horizon, melting the sky in its path in a glorious wash of colors as "You and Me" by Lifehouse wafted from the wireless speaker we'd propped in front of the door. Castiel shook his head as he watched me spread out the wide array of treats that we'd lugged up to the roof. I'd left the apartment at the crack of dawn that morning, just long enough to stock up on all the foods that I would want if I only had three days on earth.

I selected a perfectly ripened strawberry from the plastic container on the blanket in front of me, and

Castiel eyed me warily as I held it out to him. "I am still not sure what the point of this is."

"You said you wanted memories of human sensations to take back to the spiritual plane with you," I replied with a playful smirk, "Taste is a powerful sensation for us humans. Just try a bite."

He narrowed his eyes at the suspicious piece of fruit as he took it from my hand. "I suppose if you insist—"

"I *do* insist," I whispered, "Just trust me."

I held my breath as I watched his teeth sink into the berry in question. Cramming a whole lifetime's worth of memories into a few short days was no easy task, and I really didn't want to disappoint him.

A thin trickle of berry juice dripped from his bottom lip and he wiped it away with his free hand as he closed his eyes, savoring the fruit in his mouth as if he had all the time in the world to finish it. As he swallowed the first bite of food that he'd ever eaten, he opened his eyes and met my expectant gaze with an expression that I couldn't quite decipher.

"I can't read you," I muttered, "Did you like it?"

A wide grin spread across his face as he nodded. "I had no idea that flavors could be so *intense.*"

I wasn't sure whether I should deflate at his sarcastic jab or beam with pride over my successful choice. "Are you messing with me?"

"No," he muttered, pausing midsentence to pop the rest of the berry in his mouth before adding, "I mean it."

I picked up the box of assorted chocolates sitting beside the storage crate that we'd used to lug all our picnic supplies up to the roof. "If you think that was good," I murmured as I opened the box and held it out to him so he could choose a piece for himself, "then you should try one of these."

He studied the contents for several seconds before selecting a round piece of dark chocolate from the center of the box. As he bit into it, a hushed groan rumbled deep in his throat.

I watched him chew the chocolate, slowly and deliberately with a rapturous glint in his eyes, and a triumphant grin spread across my face as I selected a chocolate for myself and sat the box down between us. "Even better than the strawberry?"

"I never truly grasped the meaning of the word delicious until just now," he muttered with a nod.

"Good," I whispered, "I'm glad you like the food. I was afraid you might not be able to taste it like I do."

A knowing grin tugged at the corners of his mouth as he selected another piece of chocolate from the box. "You were worried it might all just taste like molecules?"

An unintentional chuckle hiccupped from my mouth at his offhand reference to my favorite show. I *had* been worried that I might be wasting his time with food that he wouldn't even be able to taste. "How did you—"

"You keep forgetting," he muttered around the chocolate in his mouth, "I have always been with you, Abigail. I have watched every episode of *Supernatural* that you have."

"So, you've watched *all* of them," I muttered with a sheepish grin, "more than once."

He nodded, then eyed the box between us. "What exactly is the appropriate etiquette in this situation?"

I raised an eyebrow as I took a second piece of chocolate from the box. "What do you mean?"

"Gluttony is a sin," he muttered, "and I believe it is also socially frowned upon."

My cheeks flamed with embarrassment as his eyes met mine. "If you've been beside me during everything, you've seen me devour chocolates without giving so much as a passing thought to *etiquette.*"

The angel's carefree laughter was music to my ears. "I am not beside you to judge."

"Yes, you are," I muttered as I dropped my eyes to the chocolates, "How could you lead me down the right path if you didn't judge my actions as right or wrong?"

He grinned at me as I looked back up at him. "I do not believe any soul was ever denied access to heaven for eating too many helpings of dessert."

I frowned at him with mock frustration. "Didn't you just say that gluttony was a sin?"

He let out another chuckle. "Gluttony implies an excess that I do not believe you are capable of."

"I don't know why we're even debating this," I muttered, "Eat the whole box. I bought them for you. I can get another box for myself after..." The music seemed to swell as my voice trailed off, unable to finish the sentence.

I turned toward the sky to hide the tears that filled my eyes. The sun was almost gone now, and the sunset it had left in its wake was more brilliant than any I'd ever witnessed before. Another day with my angel was coming to a close. The day after tomorrow would be the last of them. Two more sunsets didn't seem like nearly enough.

I turned back to Castiel. That ancient sorrow that had darkened his eyes while he was sharing his story with me stared back at me from the infinite depths of his angelic eyes.

Was it possible that he was just as heartbroken that our time together was coming to an end? I wanted to ask him to stay just a few more days, but I hadn't forgotten his words when I'd first asked him to stay. He was afraid that the longer he stayed with me like this, the harder it would be for him to leave. *Please don't go.* The silent plea teetered on the tip of my tongue, begging to be spoken. But I couldn't say it out loud. I had vowed to do everything I could to help him earn his place back in heaven. Still, I couldn't stop the thought from screaming inside my head. *Please don't leave me here alone.* I wasn't ready to let him go, and I wasn't sure how I would manage to go on living after he left me.

Time seemed to stop as we sat there staring into each other's eyes. *He didn't want to leave.* I could see it in his eyes—the longing for more time, the heartache that flared at the thought of our time together coming to an end.

A tear slid down my cheek as I forced a smile. "Could you guide me down a path that leads to heaven sooner?"

"That is not how it works," he replied in a hoarse whisper, "You must use all the time you are given to make a difference in the lives of others."

My eyes drifted to the darkening sky as I muttered, "I could still do that if you stayed here with me."

"I wish I could," he whispered, "but that is not how it's done."

"It could be..." My voice trailed off as I met his eyes and watched them darken a bit more.

"No," he whispered, "that path would not lead to heaven."

"I already told you," I croaked as I blinked back my tears, "for as long as you're with me, heaven is right here on earth."

The music swelled, filling the silence that lingered between us as the last traces of light disappeared from the sky. That's what it would feel like when my angel disappeared. All of the light in my world would vanish right along with him, and I'd be alone in the dark...

...I could still hear "You and Me" playing in the distance as I opened my eyes in the hospital room. My childhood friend was sitting on the bed beside me. I could feel the warmth of his hand gripping mine.

"Mom," my son muttered, "Can you hear me?"

"Yes," I managed to croak.

Danny stood from his chair at my bedside and picked up the plastic cup of water on the bedside table. He dipped one of the little sponges on a stick in the water and swabbed my tongue with a gentleness that brought tears to my failing eyes. "I love you," he whispered as his own eyes filled with tears.

"I love you too," I muttered as he removed the sponge from my mouth. I couldn't see far, but I could see enough to know that Cassie was gone. It was just me and my two Dannys in the room now, with the music from my past playing softly in the distance.

My son noticed me glancing toward his sister's vacant chair. "Cassie went home to take a shower and try to get a few hours of sleep, but she'll be back soon."

I wasn't sure whether I wanted her to be there when I went. Grown as she was, Cassie would always be my baby. How could I let her witness my last breath? I knew exactly what it would do to her because my childhood friend's final breath had haunted me for years...

17

"Like Real People Do"

Hozier

W e sat on my living room floor on opposite sides of the coffee table as Hozier's "Like Real People Do" wafted from the speaker across the room. Our dirty dessert dishes were neatly stacked at the far end of the table and I was in no particular hurry to wash them, especially since they were practically spotless already. We had devoured every last crumb of the black forest cake on our plates before stacking them and shoving them aside to make room for our board games.

I shook my head as I studied the chessboard on the table in front of me. Then I slid my queen across the board, banishing one of Castiel's knights from the playing field. "This is hopeless," I muttered as I watched him demolish my favorite chess piece with a bishop that'd escaped my attention while I was moving my ill-fated queen.

Castiel grinned at me as he propped an elbow on the coffee table and lowered his chin to his fist. "What is hopeless?"

I started to pick up my rook, but let go as soon as I realized the move I was about to make would be just as doomed as my last. A playful smile spread across my face as I lifted my eyes to my angel's. "I'm thinking that playing a game of strategy with a celestial being who's been around since the dawn of creation wasn't exactly my brightest idea."

"Yes," my guardian angel replied with a hushed chuckle, "I suppose I have had a few more millennia to observe strategic maneuvers."

"Oh, a few more millennia," I muttered as I shrugged and slid my poor rook to his death, "Is that all?"

"You weren't thrilled with the outcome of our trivia game," Castiel mused, "and now you are unhappy playing chess. What would you like to try next?"

"The fact that you actually *lived* through every event in the trivia questions gave you an unfair advantage," I muttered, "but I never said I wasn't happy. As long as I'm spending time with you, I'd be happy doing just about anything."

He lifted his chin from his fist and lowered his hand to rest on top of mine with a smile that was every bit as warm as his touch. "I feel the same way about spending time with you, Abigail."

My cheeks bloomed with heat as I pushed the chessboard toward our dirty dishes with my free hand. "Let's not drag this game out. You win. So, what should we do now?"

"I leave that choice up to you," he replied in a gruff whisper.

I nodded and let the music fill the void as we both fell silent. When the silence began to feel too heavy, I let out a sigh and whispered, "Can I ask you a small question?"

Castiel's brow furrowed with interest as he murmured, "Of course."

I glanced down at his hand, resting on top of mine. "What am I supposed to be doing with my life?"

"That is no small question," he replied in a hushed tone, "It is not my place to determine your path."

"But it *is* your place to guide me in the right direction," I muttered as I looked up at him, "What's the difference?"

"I can encourage you to make adjustments to your present course and I can point out the paths ahead that it would be wise to avoid," a hint of regret crept into his gruff tone as he added, "but I cannot tell you what to do with your life. Those choices are entirely up to you."

"I'm not exactly brave or outgoing...or even confident, for that matter," I muttered as I lowered my gaze to the coffee table, "So, how am I supposed to help others and make this world a better place, when just the *thought* of putting myself out there terrifies me?"

"Why does that terrify you?" he asked in a guttural whisper that beckoned me to look up and meet his gaze.

"Because going out on a limb like that is risking rejection, and I don't handle rejection very well," I muttered in a hoarse whisper, "It brings back too many painful memories..."

Hozier's hypnotic voice seemed to grow louder as my voice trailed off, heightening the melancholy mood during the brief silence that followed my words.

After a moment, Castiel cleared his throat. "You shouldn't view your fear of rejection as a weakness. It is one of your greatest strengths."

A humorless chuckle erupted from my throat. "How on earth is my crippling fear of being rejected a *strength*?"

A smile of adoration tugged at the corners of his mouth. "Painful as it was, all of the suffering that you endured helped to shape you into the empathetic individual you are today. There are so many souls in this world who are struggling just to make it through one more day. Many of them have been hurt and have suffered through grievous injustice—and they fear rejection, just as you do. The smallest gesture of kindness can often have a profound impact on such a struggling individual's life."

"But I wouldn't have a clue what small gesture to make," I muttered with a shake of my head.

"Trust me," he whispered, "When those opportunities present themselves, you will know what to do."

"How can you be so sure?"

A sympathetic smile spread across my angel's face as he gave my hand a comforting squeeze, filling me with warmth. "In those disconcerting moments, when you witness something that doesn't seem right—and you feel as if you should step in to help—trust that quiet voice inside your head. It will always steer you in the right direction."

"That voice," I muttered, pausing to swallow the lump in my throat, "It's you, isn't it?"

"I am always beside you, Abigail," he replied with a nod, "Nudging you in the right direction during those pivotal moments is what I was placed here to do."

Unable to voice the plea that was poised on the tip of my tongue, I nodded and turned my attention to the window. The sky was beginning to darken. "We should go up to the roof to watch the sunset again. You seemed to enjoy doing that yesterday."

"I have overseen countless sunsets, since I witnessed the first of them at the dawn of creation," he murmured as he touched my cheek, "but watching the sunset with you yesterday was an altogether different experience."

"If you've always been beside me," I muttered, "then you've seen plenty of sunsets with me already, haven't you?"

"Yes," he replied, "but viewing daylight's end through human eyes, as you viewed it, was what made that particular sunset extraordinary. The wonder in your eyes was far more magnificent than any sunset could ever be."

I opened my mouth, then shut it without saying a word because I couldn't voice the only response that sprang to mind. *Please don't leave me tomorrow. Stay here with me.*

His eyes darkened as he shook his head, almost as if he knew what I wanted to say.

I would if I could, a voice inside my head whispered. I wanted to believe that those were his words; but more likely than not, it was just wishful thinking on my part. *How was I supposed to follow him down the right path, if I had no way of telling which thoughts came from him and which were nothing more than figments of my imagination?* I shook those thoughts from my head as I hopped up to grab my cell phone and portable speaker, while Castiel grabbed the blanket we'd brought up to the roof the night before.

There were no words for what I was feeling—at least, none that I could voice. We made our way up to the rooftop in silence, both of us lost in our own thoughts as we propped the door open with my portable speaker and sat down on the blanket that Castiel spread out for us.

A gentle breeze whispered through the crisp evening air as Hozier's "Like Real People Do" played from my wireless speaker, and I couldn't tell whether it was Hozier's hauntingly beautiful melody or the night air that sent a shiver down my spine.

Castiel slid closer to me and wrapped an arm around my shoulders, chasing away the chill with his warmth. I dropped my head to his shoulder, and together we watched the sunset drench the darkening sky in the most brilliant array of colors that I had ever witnessed. It felt as if the sky knew this sunset was almost our last. As stupid a thought as that was, a tear slid down my cheek as an unbearable ache seared my heart.

One more sunset, and my angel would vanish along with the sun...

18

"Hey Jude"

The Beatles

We had less than twenty-four hours left before Castiel's physical form reached its expiration date. I was trying my best to stay strong, but a weighted ball of dread was steadily growing in the pit of my stomach. With each passing hour, it seemed to drag me down a bit more. When it came time for my angel to leave, I was pretty sure it was going to drop me to the ground. I shook my head to rid those grim thoughts from my mind. That was something to worry about after he was gone. I refused to waste our final hours together mourning tomorrow's loss. He was here with me now, and I intended to enjoy every last second I had with him.

My eyes drifted toward the doorway to the kitchen as I shifted sideways on the couch. Castiel was in there fixing us one last dinner. He'd enjoyed eating the foods I introduced him to so much that he wanted to prepare a meal on his own for the two of us to share. Now that we were nearing the end of our time together, it made my heart ache just being in separate rooms. I had to keep reminding myself that my angel was just in the kitchen and I would see him again soon enough.

Damn it. I needed to do something to snap myself out of this funk so I could enjoy our final meal together. The surest way to escape my worries had always been music, *Danny's music.* So, I hopped off the couch, ran to my room and grabbed my cell phone and earbuds from the bedside table.

I pulled Danny's playlist up on my phone as I headed back down the hall toward the living room. Listening to one song on repeat didn't seem like the way to go tonight. I needed the music to be spontaneous and fluid because unexpected changes —from one song to the next—would help keep my mind off my worries better than a single song playing on an endless loop.

I popped my earbuds in my ears as I stepped into the living room. Then I put the playlist on shuffle and stuffed my phone in the front pocket of my jeans. Despite the burgeoning sense of dread that was weighing me down, I couldn't help grinning as "Hey Jude" by the Beatles began to play. Too antsy to sit still, I danced around the living room while I straightened things up to the beat of the music.

As the song grew louder, I froze midway through fluffing a pillow, closed my eyes and let the melody wash over me. Then I tossed the pillow in the general direction of the couch and just let my body move to the music. Without even realizing I was doing it, I started belting the words out as I danced like a woman possessed with my eyes squeezed shut.

A slight disturbance to the air current in the room prompted me to open my eyes, and I nearly jumped out of my skin when I found Castiel standing just a few feet in front of me. He was watching me through narrowed eyes with his head cocked to one side, in that ever-endearing way of his that so perfectly mimicked my favorite television angel. Heat rushed to my face as I let out a laugh and tugged the earpiece out of my right ear.

His brow furrowed with confusion as he muttered, "Did I do something amusing?"

"No," I whispered, fighting the urge to look away as I felt my blush deepen, "I'm just embarrassed that you caught me in the act."

He cocked his head a bit more to the side as the corners of his mouth turned down in a quizzical frown. "The act of *what?*"

Oblivious to the interruption of my dance party, the Beatles continued to serenade me in my left ear as I shrugged and muttered, "The act of *dancing*, I guess."

Castiel nodded but looked no less confused.

I flashed him a sympathetic smile. "What are you thinking?"

"I have never understood why humans are so moved by music," he muttered as his eyes searched mine.

"Music is the closest thing that we have to magic," I confided in a reverent whisper, "because it has the power to anchor us to a moment in time."

His half-smile conveyed a heartwarming mix of curiosity and affection. "How so?"

I felt my face flush a shade darker as I grinned at him. "When we hear a song from our past, it conjures up all the old sensations that we felt when we first heard it."

He eyed me with a perplexed frown as he took a step toward me. "How can a combination of man-made instruments and human vocal chords wield that sort of power?"

"I can't explain it with words," I whispered, "It's something that you just have to *feel*."

He stood there staring at me with that puzzled expression on his face as I stepped closer and carefully inserted the earpiece in my hand into his left ear, so the music connected the two of us, just as surely as the cord connected the earbuds in our ears. "Maybe you'd understand what I mean if you danced to the music."

"I don't dance," he muttered as he watched me begin to sway to the beat.

I smiled at him as I took his hands in mine and moved his arms in time with the music, like a puppeteer pulling a life-sized marionette's strings. "Anyone can dance. You just have to let go and let the music guide your movements."

A skeptical frown spread across his face as he watched me, but he let me direct his movements nonetheless. He was stiff and awkward at first but as the music grew louder, he seemed to find the rhythm. "These words are nonsense," he muttered.

"Shhh," I whispered, "Don't think. Just feel."

He was a remarkably fast learner, but I suppose being on earth since the dawn of time had given him plenty of opportunities to watch humans dance. Once he started to *feel* the music, he moved with all the grace that you'd imagine an angel would.

"Hey Jude" gradually faded away until there was nothing but silence in our twin earpieces.

We stopped moving and stood there staring at each other while we waited for the next song to guide our movements.

19

"World Spins Madly On"
The Weepies

Silence crackled in the air between us as we stood motionless in the center of my living room, and the power of speech temporarily escaped me as his eyes locked with mine. There was a fierce intensity to this silence, almost as if the whole world were holding its breath for us. I found myself longing to preserve the moment and carry it with me till the day my heart stopped beating.

A shiver raced down my spine as "World Spins Madly On" by the Weepies began to play in our ears.

Castiel smiled at me as he took my right hand in his left and placed his other hand on my waist with the nonchalant confidence of a well-seasoned dance partner.

An involuntary grin spread across my face as I put my free hand on his shoulder, and we let the music take control. For some stupid reason, I took great pleasure in knowing that any onlooker would hear nothing but silence as they watched us dance. *This song was connecting the two of us.* It played for no one else.

I was stunned by the effortless fluidity of my angelic dance partner's movements as he twirled me around the living room in perfect time to the morbidly cheery tune. Although, I'm not exactly sure why his grace came as such a shock. He'd had thousands of years to observe the movements of graceful dancers. I suppose it just caught me off guard because it was such a far cry from the television angel's awkward mannerisms, but as expertly as he played the part, he wasn't really the fictional angel from *Supernatural.* He was *my* angel.

An ache flared in my chest as I listened to the song's heartbreaking lyrics. *This dance would have to last me a lifetime.* I dropped my head to his shoulder and willed my mind to sear the feel of this moment into my senses forever.

I could tell that Castiel felt it too—how close we were to the end of our time together, and how precious this moment was—because he tightened his grip on me and touched his head to mine as we moved to the music that connected us as one.

I breathed in deep, desperate to commit his scent to memory. He smelled like my grandmother's gingerbread, fresh from the oven...the pleasant scent of pipe tobacco that used to cling to my grandfather's shirts...the blend of exotic spices that always lingered in the kitchen at my friend Danny's house...and what I imagined sunshine would smell like, if the sun had a scent. *He smelled like happiness.* My heart throbbed at the thought of spending the remainder of my life without him.

As the music swelled, Castiel lifted me off the floor and spun us around in a circle. It was such a joyful spontaneous movement that a burst of laughter sprang from my mouth as my eyes met his. The smile that spread across his face filled me with warmth as the singers' voices rose and fell. He spun us around in repetitive circles in perfect time with the music, while I giggled like a silly school girl without a care in the world. He stopped spinning right on cue with the change in verse. Then he lowered me to my feet and dipped me.

Entirely confident that he would never let me drop, I surrendered to the moment and fell back in his arms.

He gently tugged me upright just as the music reached a crescendo, and my breath caught in my throat as our eyes met. Something foreign was staring back at me from the depths of his ancient blue eyes. I wasn't quite sure what it was, or why it made my heart hammer in my chest the way it did. All I knew for certain, was that I never wanted this moment to end.

The room seemed to spin around us as the instrumental section of the song played on while we stood perfectly still in the center. "I get it now," Castiel murmured, heating me with the warmth of his breath as the words left his lips.

I leaned back in his arms, just enough to get a better look at him. "You get *what*?"

The anguish in his eyes made my heart skip a beat as he muttered, "Why the other Watchers took human wives."

The floor beneath my feet seemed to lose its solidity as his words shattered every trace of protective armor that had shielded my heart through years of sorrow. "And I understand why those women sacrificed eternity for a few short years with their angels," I muttered in a breathless whisper.

Tears shimmered in his eyes as he let go of my hand and brushed his fingertips over my cheek.

And my heart stopped beating.

His comforting touch had always warmed me, *but never like this.* The warmth at my cheek from that slight touch of his fingers heated the blood that rushed through my veins and spread through my body, setting my insides on fire—and I knew that if he left me now, I would never survive.

Tears filled my eyes as I lifted a trembling hand to his face. I touched his cheek and traced the strong line of his jaw with my fingers, desperate to commit every feature of his angelic face to memory. "I don't want..." A single tear slid down my cheek as my breath hitched, and the strength to finish that sentence escaped me.

He dipped his head and touched his forehead to mine. He had done that before *but this time, it felt entirely different.* He brushed his thumb across my cheek to wipe away the tear and every nerve ending in my body burst into flames. It was a wonder I didn't combust on the spot. *How had the wives of the Watchers survived their angel's touch?* It didn't seem possible. Any more contact than this, and I would forget how to function—my lungs would forget how to take in air and my heart would forget to how to beat—and yet, *I wanted more.* In that moment, I would have gladly signed a crossroad demon's contract—pledging my soul to eternal damnation in exchange for just one night with this angel—without even hesitating to think it over.

He exhaled a sigh of frustration, bathing me in his warmth. "Promise me something?"

"Anything," I agreed in a hushed rasp.

Eons of suffering darkened his eyes as he whispered, "Do not ever doubt how precious you are."

I tried to promise him, but my throat seemed incapable of producing a sound. Instead, I nodded against his forehead, thrilling at each new inch of contact between us as my forehead slid against his. Was he still leaving me? *How could I convince him to change his mind?*

"Never doubt," his voice cracked midsentence and he stopped to take a breath before whispering, "how precious you are to me."

"Alright," I managed to mutter. I wanted to beg him to stay. I wanted to tell him that I'd never be able to go on without him, but my throat refused to voice the words.

"Live your life doing good for others, Abigail," he murmured as he wiped a fresh tear from my cheek, "Look for every small opportunity to make a difference in someone else's life."

"I will," I managed to croak, but inside I was screaming. *Please don't leave me! I'll never survive without you!*

The song ended the second I agreed to do as he asked, and the finality of the silence that followed weighed down on me, crushing me until I couldn't breathe.

20

"Can't Help Falling in Love"
Elvis Presley

A s I stood there staring into the eyes of my angel with my heart crumbling inside my chest, the absoluteness of the silence between us choked the air from my lungs. The look in his eyes was unreadable. I desperately wanted to believe that he was changing his mind, *that I could convince him to stay.*

The moment Elvis's "Can't Help Falling in Love" shattered the silence, a broken sob escaped my throat; and for the first time, I questioned the validity of Castiel's statement that random song selections were meaningless.

He pulled me closer and kissed the top of my head, all but igniting me in flames. Then he took my hand in his, and we started dancing around the room again at an unhurried pace that fit the dreamy tempo of the song.

I dropped my head to his shoulder and did my best to suppress my tears. Focusing on the song's lyrics certainly didn't help. It felt like the song had been written for this precise moment in time—as if a celestial being had whispered in Elvis's ear when he wrote it—so that one day, this song could speak directly to us.

God forgive me. I didn't care what happened to my soul. I wanted my angel to stay with me, even if both of us would burn for it in the end. Eternal damnation seemed like a small price to pay.

Castiel pulled me closer and as he touched his head to mine, I felt something cosmic shift. We didn't seem to be moving to the music any longer. We were standing still. *I could feel the earth spinning.* I could feel his heart beating, and I knew without a doubt that he wanted to stay, just as badly as I wanted him to. Somehow, I knew in that instant that one whispered plea from me was all it would take to convince him to stay. I tried to speak, but all that came out was a breathless sob.

He drew me tighter against him as the world spun around us. I can't explain what was happening logically. We were dancing without moving, while the stationary room spun around us, as the king of rock-and-roll crooned his perfect love song in our ears.

One simple word would bind him to me until both of us burned.

My heart hammered in my chest as I willed my throat to produce the word—*Stay.* That was all I needed to say. *But what if I said it and he left me anyway?* I knew I could never recover from that blow. *Was it better to leave it like this than to risk the possibility of him rejecting me?* No. How could I *not* take that risk?

Stay.

Time seemed to have stopped moving for the two of us because the song had gone on much longer than it should have. I wanted it to keep playing forever. As long as we stayed—suspended in this moment—there was no heartbreak, no devastation as he left me alone for the rest of my days.

He'd still be with me in a spiritual sense after he vanished, but that wouldn't be the same. I had felt the whispered echo of his touch in the past. *It was nothing like this.* Dancing in his arms was like nothing I had ever experienced, and I knew nothing would ever surpass this moment. *This was my heaven.* What better place could possibly await me in the afterlife?

Stay.

I hugged him tighter, desperate to keep him there with me. Had Danny known somehow? Had he foreseen my future while he was creating his playlist for me? The songs all seemed to fit my life so perfectly, *too perfectly* to be just a coincidence.

Stay.

I felt the warmth of a tear that wasn't mine drip down the side of my face, and my throat constricted around the plea that I was desperate to utter.

Castiel had resisted when all the other Watchers were defiling themselves with human women all those years ago. *He hadn't even been tempted.* So, I had to be misinterpreting his actions. He couldn't possibly be considering condemning himself to hell for *me* when he'd never even understood his brothers' unforgivable choices.

I felt another one of his tears slip down my cheek as his mouth dropped to my ear. He hugged me tighter and whispered, "You are precious, Abigail."

Of course. He sensed how hopelessly I'd fallen for him, how desperately I wanted him to stay. *He was just trying to let me down easy.* That was the only logical explanation for his tears and his whispered words.

"Don't you dare doubt my feelings for you," he whispered in my ear, "You *are* that precious, Abigail."

I wanted to ask what he meant by *that* precious. *Precious enough to regret leaving? Precious enough to commit an unforgivable sin for?*

There was no doubt in my mind that this song had gone on much longer than it should have and yet, it played on. Elvis kept on toying with my heart as our eternal fate hung in the balance.

Castiel stopped dancing and stood still as the king of rock-and-roll continued to serenade us. He was holding me so close that I had no choice but to stop moving with him. I turned my head to look at him, and my heart stuttered as our eyes met. I wanted to ask him what exactly he'd meant when he called me precious, but I couldn't remember how to speak. I could barely remember to *breathe*.

He let go of my hand and it instantly felt ice cold without his warmth. Then he smiled at me as he lifted his hand to my face. He brushed his fingertips over my tear-stained cheek, then drew my head closer as he lowered his head.

I watched his mouth inch closer, terrified to move or dare to assume that he was lowering those perfect lips to my mouth. When his lips touched mine, I burst into tears as he kissed me slowly and deeply with the utmost tenderness while the world spun around us.

I had lived with Collin for years and when he made love to me, it had always been magical. But this angel's kiss surpassed anything I'd ever experienced in the throes of passion. My heart was pounding, my soul was singing and my entire body was ablaze. *I was tasting heaven.*

Just like the song, the kiss seemed to go on forever. I wasn't sure what message the kiss was meant to convey. *I'll stay? Goodbye?* But I didn't care. I was melting in his angelic arms, praying for this kiss to stop my heart so that I could leave this world along with him.

When his lips pulled away from mine, I felt my heart shatter.

He touched his forehead to mine as the song ended, and his ancient eyes shimmered with tears as he whispered, "You are precious." Then he lifted me off the floor and carried me toward my bedroom.

I was speechless. All I could do was keep my eyes locked with his and hope that my face conveyed all the love I felt for him. *He already knew.* He'd said it himself, the day I found him sitting on the couch in my living room, *he was everything to me.* He always had been.

He placed me on the bed with such care, as if I were made of glass and he was afraid he might break me.

Tears slid down my cheeks as he laid down on the bed beside me and touched a hand to my cheek.

Then the world went dark...

...The song was still playing as I resurfaced in the present. My childhood friend was sitting beside me on the bed, and my son was hunched over in the chair he'd dragged to my bedside. He was slumped against my legs, fast asleep.

My dear friend smiled at me as I met his eyes.

Did you always know?

His smile deepened. *That the songs on my playlist would conform so perfectly to the events of your life?*

I smiled as widely as my cracked lips would allow me to. *Yes.*

Not completely, **he replied with a subtle shake of his head,** *but it did feel like something or someone was guiding my song choices.*

A searing pain ripped through my insides, and a tear slid down my cheek as I suppressed a scream. I didn't want to wake my son, especially not in such a jarring manner.

Danny leaned closer to me and brushed my cheek with his fingertips, as if to wipe away the tear. I could feel the warmth of my friend's touch, but the tear remained on my cheek. *Let me take you now, Abbie. Your kids will be okay. They have each other to lean on.*

I managed to turn my head enough to look at my son, slumped over beside my legs. They're not ready. I can't leave them yet.

Then you should rest. **My dear friend planted a kiss on my wrinkled cheek, and I drifted back to the past...**

21

"In My Place"

Coldplay

---

s I drifted toward consciousness the next morning, Coldplay's "In My Place" was playing on repeat in the earbuds that were now wedged in both my ears. My heart was crumbling inside my chest, *and my angel was gone.*

I jolted upright on the bed, gasping for breath with my heart racing as my eyes frantically searched the room. *There was no trace of Castiel,* no sign that he'd ever actually been there at all.

Dread churned in the pit of my stomach as I scrambled out of bed and raced through room after room of my apartment, searching for him. With each empty room, the dreadful feeling intensified— spreading through my body like a cancerous growth, disabling me little by little—until it crept up my throat, making it nearly impossible to breathe.

When I reached the empty living room, I stopped dead in my tracks as I eyed the doorway to the kitchen. That was the only room left to check, but I didn't have to look. I knew he wasn't in there. The quiet in my apartment was too absolute. It felt too empty.

Coldplay's cruel words rang in my ears, taunting me as my breath escaped me in an agonized rush, and I dropped to my knees on the living room carpet. *He was gone.* Massive gut-wrenching sobs shook my body as I curled up in a ball on the living room floor. Desperate to feel anything that might blunt the unbearable ache in my chest, I tugged at fistfuls of my hair. The ache didn't subside at all, but the jolt of pain helped jog a thought to the forefront of my brain. Castiel had been cooking dinner for our last night together. *The dinner that he was preparing should still be in my kitchen.* At the very least, I needed to find some sort of proof that I hadn't imagined the last three days of my life, *the best three days of my life.*

I dried the tears from my cheeks with my shirtsleeve as I stood up from the floor. Then I inched toward the kitchen with my heart in my throat. What would I do if there was nothing in there to prove that Castiel had been real?

I held my breath as I stepped through the doorway, and my stomach dropped.

There was no meal, no ingredients for our final dinner, not a single dirty pot or pan, not even a note to explain why he'd left so abruptly. There was nothing at all to prove that he'd ever been anything more than a figment of my delusional imagination.

My stomach lurched as the realization that *I had imagined all of it* sunk in, and I raced to the bathroom in a cold sweat. In my rush to reach the toilet in time, I didn't bother to shut the door behind me. But what did it matter? There was no one around to witness my actions, no one to care how low I had sunk.

I dropped to my knees in front of the toilet, barely noticing the pain as my kneecaps collided with the unforgiving floor tiles. The moment I lifted the lid, the contents of my stomach burned their way up my throat...

...My wrinkled cheeks were slick with tears, and my heart was pounding so hard that I could hear its frantic beat echoing in my ears as I resurfaced in the hospital room. Thanks to the massive adrenaline rush that'd propelled me out of the past, desperate to escape that agony, I had no trouble opening my eyes this time.

My childhood friend greeted me with a sympathetic smile.

I opened my mouth to speak, but closed it when I remembered that my throat was too dry to produce much sound. I don't want to remember the rest.

Danny reached over and took my hand in his. Trust me, Abbie. You don't want to end on that note.

I squeezed my eyes shut. Please, Danny. I can't relive any more of that heartbreak.

He shifted sideways on the bed, so we were face to face. I can take you away from all of this pain. Are you ready to say goodbye to your children now?

I was so afraid of leaving before Cassie was ready to let me go that I actually mustered the strength to shake my head. No, not yet. *Another tidal wave of pain ripped through my insides and my body instinctively went rigid, bracing itself against the unbearable ache.*

Danny leaned forward and touched his forehead to mine. It's too painful for you to stay here now, Abbie. If you aren't ready to move on yet, you need to go back to the past. Why don't we just skip ahead a little, so you don't have to relive all that heartache?

I wanted to protest and stay in the present where my children were, but the pain was far too intense. Alright.

The instant I consented, the past reclaimed me...

...It took me a long while to come to grips with the truth, but eventually I had to accept the fact that I'd suffered a complete mental breakdown after

Collin's death. At least, that was my conclusion based on my extensive internet research. Of course, I knew you shouldn't self-diagnose something that major, but I was too terrified to mention what had happened to anyone. I'd veered so far from sanity that I was afraid they might lock me up and throw away the key if I sought professional help. Thankfully, everyone just assumed that it was the death of my ex-boyfriend that'd reduced me to the human equivalent of a train-wreck, and I certainly didn't correct their assumptions. I figured that was a far more acceptable explanation than mourning the loss of a fictional character, I'd deluded myself into believing I was hanging out with for days.

After months of wallowing in my own misery, I decided I had no choice but to accept what had happened and move on. What other options did I have, aside from trying to kill myself again? *That is, if I'd ever actually tried to begin with.* For all I knew, I might have hallucinated that whole scenario with the sleeping pills in my kitchen. Either way, it was time for me to stop obsessing over what had *or hadn't* happened and get on with my life.

My first step toward moving on was to start attending N.A. meetings on a regular basis again. I vowed to go to at least one a week. I didn't divulge what had happened to turn me into such a diehard regular at the Thursday night meetings, but just going and being a silent member of the group helped me muster the strength to move forward.

I went back to college the next fall and I stuck with it until I earned my teaching degree. Judy let me keep on renting the apartment for next to nothing while I was a student. In fact, I decided to stay even after I graduated, once I convinced her to raise the rent to a price that was fairer to her. I didn't want to take advantage of Judy's kindness, but I also didn't want to move. After all that time, the apartment had begun to feel like home and although I'd never admit it—*even to myself*—I couldn't bear the thought of leaving the place that held such wonderful memories of my time with Castiel.

As luck would have it, I found a teaching position at a nearby elementary school soon after graduation. Teaching my class of first graders filled my heart with joy to the point of bursting. They were so kindhearted and pure at that age. Although, a part of me couldn't help wishing that I could shield every less-than-perfect child, the ones that were inevitably destined to be tormented by schoolyard predators in the future. I would have given anything to protect them from the cruelty that awaited them in the years ahead, but I had to settle for showering them with the attention they deserved and praying they'd never doubt how precious they truly were.

After a while my work days began to blur together, but they were enjoyable days. Life was pretty darn good and I didn't want to risk stumbling off the path, so I still made it a priority to attend an N.A. meeting every week.

Decades later, I still thanked God for that. I could only imagine how different my life might have been if I hadn't been there that night…

…It was a rainy Thursday evening. Despite my reluctance to leave the apartment and head out in such dreary weather, I decided it wasn't wise to tempt fate. Things were going so well in my structured little life. I didn't want to jinx that by skipping my weekly N.A. meeting. I knew myself. Skipping one would just make it easier for me to convince myself that it was okay to skip more.

I'd procrastinated leaving my nice warm apartment for so long that the meeting had already started by the time I got there. I slipped in the room, quietly shut the door behind me and chose a seat near the back, hoping to go unnoticed and slip out as soon my obligatory hour was over.

New faces were nothing out of the ordinary at these meetings. People came and went all the time according to their needs, so I didn't pay much attention to the new girl who was sitting two seats over from me until she stood up to speak. She had a baby-faced look of innocence about her that seemed extremely out of place at a Narcotics Anonymous meeting. Her clothes were a bit on the shabby side; and as she moved toward me, I couldn't help noticing that she carried herself with the unmistakable cowering posture of a creature of prey. Seeing something of my younger self in her, I flashed her an encouraging smile as she slipped past me to get to the aisle.

The gratitude in her eyes for that one fleeting gesture of acceptance tugged at my heartstrings and captured my full attention.

The girl's name was Brandy. She was only eighteen years-old and her story of hardship made mine seem like a fairytale in comparison. She ran away from home at the age of sixteen to get away from an abusive stepfather, and things didn't get much better for her on the streets. My eyes welled with tears as she told us about the delinquent runaways she fell in with when she first got to the city, and the things she ended up doing to pay for the heroin that they got her hooked on. She dropped her eyes to the floor as she explained that she was determined to leave all of that behind and commit herself to getting clean for the sake of the baby she was now carrying. Brandy was desperate to give her baby a better childhood than her own.

As I listened to her story, a conversation I had with Castiel during my temporary break from sanity came to mind. I'd worked so hard to erect mental walls around those memories and convince myself that those three days had never happened, but I couldn't help thinking of the angel's advice to me now. *Look for every small opportunity to make a difference in someone else's life.* I knew what it was like to feel all alone in this cold cruel world. So, as tired and anxious to get home as I was, I decided to hang back after the meeting and introduce myself to Brandy because it seemed like she could really use a friend.

When the meeting ended, I stayed in my seat and watched Brandy head to the table of coffee and cookies at the back of the room. As I stood up and made my way toward the table, I watched her glance around self-consciously, then fill her paper plate with cookies. The cookies that they put out at those meetings were nothing to write home about, but judging by the way Brandy eyed them, I got the feeling she was used to going hungry.

I kept my distance as I reached the table and tried to decide how to approach her. I wasn't exactly an extrovert. For me, making new friends was an awkward process that brought me right back to my childhood, when every new face had been a potential predator just waiting to pounce on a timid imperfect creature like me. *But this wasn't about me.* This was about seizing an opportunity to make a difference in somebody else's life. Even though my guardian angel had turned out to be a figment of my imagination, his message was sound.

I did my best to quiet my nerves as I approached Brandy while she was helping herself to a cup of decaf coffee. "The coffee is pretty crappy here," I muttered in a disappointingly unsteady voice.

She looked up at me and smiled with that same gratitude in her eyes that I'd witnessed when she passed by my chair. "Thanks for the warning."

I nodded as I glanced toward the window. The rain had let up quite a bit and the sky looked a little less dismal. "You know, there's a diner around the corner that I sometimes like to go to for dinner after these meetings. The coffee's a lot better there."

Her grin widened as she dropped her eyes to the half-filled cup of coffee in her hand.

She certainly didn't look like a predator. Then again, my instincts weren't always the greatest. Regardless of my subpar survival instincts, I steeled my nerves and muttered, "Would you like to join me for dinner? It'd be nice to have some company, so the waitresses don't look at me like I'm a pathetic stray puppy."

Brandy let out an uneasy laugh as her cheeks flushed with color. "That sounds nice, but I didn't bring any cash with me."

"My treat," I replied, with a confidence that I didn't actually possess.

"Thanks," she muttered as her eyes dropped to the plate of cookies on the table in front of her, "but I couldn't…"

"You would actually be doing me a favor," I whispered as I watched her falter for an excuse, "A member of the group took me out to dinner after my first meeting, back when I was scared to death to be here. Her kindness meant the world to me, and I've always wanted to pay it forward."

She stared at the coffee cup in her hand for a moment as she thought it over. Then she nodded and tucked her cup behind a plastic container full of sugar and artificial sweetener packets. "If you're sure…"

"I am," I replied as my eyes drifted back to the window. "It looks like there's a little break in the rain right now. I think this is probably our best chance to walk over there without getting drenched."

Her cheeks blushed a shade darker as she smiled at me. "Okay, you talked me into it."

It felt so good to put a smile on someone else's face that I couldn't help grinning as I pointed to the plate of cookies on the table in front of her. "The diner has much better desserts too."

She picked up the plate and nodded as she dumped her cookies back on the serving tray. I might have misread her expression, but I thought I detected a hint of gratitude for not commenting on how many she'd taken.

Brandy and I hit it off so well over dinner that I put myself out there even further and offered to be her N.A. sponsor. This time, she accepted my offer without any hesitation.

The after-meeting dinners became a regular thing for us—although after that first night, we went to Judy's diner. It was fairly obvious that Brandy was hurting for money, so I told her that Judy didn't charge fellow N.A. members for dinner on meeting nights. Thankfully, Judy was gracious enough to go along with it and let me pay her the next day. I didn't want any recognition for treating Brandy to dinner, and I certainly didn't want to make her feel embarrassed about me paying for her meals.

A little over a month into our friendship, I asked Judy if she would consider hiring Brandy as a waitress. Kind-hearted woman that she was, Judy offered her a job straightaway and she sent Brandy home with containers of food after almost every shift.

The more time Brandy and I spent together, the more comfortable she seemed to be with me. When she asked me to go along to her first ultrasound appointment, I was honored. I took the day off from work and took Brandy out to dinner afterwards to celebrate the fact that she was the mother-to-be of a healthy baby boy. I was so proud of the way Brandy had turned her life around and I was thrilled to be there to support her in any way that I could.

Brandy was just over two months shy of her due date when tragedy struck...

...I had barely gotten in the door of my apartment after a long day of parent-teacher conferences when my cell phone started ringing. I dropped my tote bag and jacket in the nearest armchair and fished my phone out of my purse just in time to answer before the call went to voicemail. "Hello?"

"Hello," the unfamiliar female voice on the other end of the line replied, "may I speak to Abigail Perkins?"

"This is Abigail," I muttered as I mentally kicked myself for answering what was obviously a telemarketer's call. Easy prey that I was, I didn't even have the guts to hang up on a pushy salesperson.

"I am so sorry to tell you this," the saleswoman replied, "but I'm calling from Saint Benedict's Hospital because Brandy Meyers has you listed as her emergency contact."

My stomach dropped at the word *hospital*. It was too soon for Brandy to go into labor. "Is Brandy alright?"

"No, I'm afraid not," the woman replied in a softer tone, "She overdosed on heroin this afternoon and her condition is critical. How fast can you get here?"

I was already heading for the door. "Twenty minutes if I can find a cab quick enough."

"Don't waste any time." The hint of desperation in the woman's tone quickened my pulse as she added, "Go straight to the Emergency Department as soon as you get here."

I'm not even sure whether I thought to say goodbye before ending the call and rushing out the door of my apartment.

It took me forever to hail a stupid cab. Thirty-eight minutes after hanging up with the woman, who I now wished to God *had* been a telemarketer, I rushed through the entrance to the Emergency Department of Saint Benedict's Hospital.

A plump older woman with a dreadfully impatient scowl was seated at the front desk.

Under normal circumstances, I would have been intimidated by her unfriendly demeanor but there was no time to think about myself. I rushed right up to her and said, "I'm here to see Brandy Meyers. I'm her emergency contact and the woman who called told me not to waste any time."

The woman's face fell as soon as I mentioned Brandy. She recovered her composure almost instantly, but my heart was already in my throat. "I'll call for someone to take you back, dear," she replied with a sympathetic smile that only amplified my worry.

Now that I had finally stopped racing toward my destination, the terror that I'd been suppressing since I received the call enveloped me. My eyes glazed over and my brain tuned out as the woman behind the desk picked up the phone and called for someone to come out and get me. I couldn't tell you what she said or how long it took for somebody to come out.

The next thing I knew, a young woman in scrubs with her hair pinned up in a haphazard knot was stepping out from behind the ominous double doors that led to the patient area behind the front desk. "Abigail?"

I blinked my eyes to bring the world back into focus as I muttered, "Yes."

I blanked for a few more minutes after that, but somehow I ended up on the other side of those double doors where a soft-spoken doctor with a foreign accent that I couldn't place was explaining things that my brain refused to process.

"I don't understand," I muttered as tears streamed down my cheeks, "Brandy was doing so well."

"From what I could gather when they first brought her in," the doctor replied with a sympathetic frown, "She ran into someone from her past."

What exactly that meant, I never did find out. Whoever it was that provided Brandy with the heroin that killed her left right after placing a frantic anonymous 911 call.

The soft-spoken doctor had miraculously managed to save Brandy's baby. Her orphaned son entered the world entirely alone, almost two months before he was due.

When the woman in scrubs who'd walked me through the double doors asked, "Would you like to come see the baby?" I was sure I must have heard her wrong.

How could she be so callous? *Why would I want to see Brandy's dead unborn child?* "Is…" comprehension slowly sunk in as I muttered, "Is the baby still…alive?"

The woman's eyes filled with tears as she smiled and whispered, "Yes, he is."

The woman in scrubs patiently explained what I'd been in too much shock to grasp the first time as she led me down a sterile hallway and onto an elevator. "The baby will have to stay in the hospital for a while…" she repeated as she pushed the button for the fourth floor, "…he needs to be kept in an incubator and he will require a lot of special care…" she continued as we stepped off the elevator and headed down another hallway. "…there will be some complications…because he was born nearly two months premature…"

The woman's voice faded to nothing more than nonsensical background noise as we entered a brightly lit room with three babies in what I assumed were the incubators she'd mentioned.

My heart hammered in my chest as I followed her to the farthest incubator from the door.

"…Premature infants tend to thrive with kangaroo care," the nurse explained as she pointed to the tiny helpless infant connected to a daunting bundle of tubes and wires.

My eyes filled with tears at the sight of the child that my friend Brandy would never get to hold in her arms. The poor thing was so fragile and small, and he was all alone in this great big terrifying world.

"...would you be interested?" The woman in scrubs smiled at me as she waited for an answer to yet another question that my brain hadn't registered.

"I'm sorry," I muttered as my eyes drifted back to Brandy's baby, "Would I be interested...in what?"

"Kangaroo care."

She said that, like it should mean something to me. I'd obviously missed most of what she'd said again. I swallowed back a sob and muttered, "I'm um...I apologize. I guess I'm having a little trouble processing all of this. What exactly is kangaroo care again?"

The woman's knowing eyes and kind smile made me feel less awful about missing everything that she'd told me twice. "It's normal to feel overwhelmed in situations like this. Kangaroo care is basically snuggle time for premature infants. The skin to skin contact helps them to thrive."

And she was asking *me* if I'd like to snuggle with this tiny helpless creature? Who was I to him? *Was that even allowed?* "I'm not a relative," I muttered as I lifted my eyes to the woman's.

"You were his mommy's emergency contact," the woman whispered, "That means, you're the closest thing to a relative that this little guy has."

"So...it's alright if I want to hold him?"

The woman in scrubs pulled a drawer beside the incubator open and took out a hospital gown. Then she held it out to me as if I were a toddler who needed help getting dressed. "Yes, it's very alright."

I obediently slipped the gown over my clothes with her help and let her guide me to a nearby rocking chair. As I dropped into it, the woman went back and disconnected the baby from the equipment in his incubator. Then she carried him over and gently placed him in my arms, close to my chest.

I knew the instant I held him in my arms.

As I snuggled this helpless infant close to my heart, my angel's words came back to me with crystal clarity—it's impossible to be something to everyone but *you can be everything to someone.*

This fragile newborn creature had no one. As he nestled contentedly against me, I knew I had found my purpose...

...I winced at the light as I resurfaced in the hospital room in the present. My son stood up from his chair at my bedside, walked to the light switches on the

wall by the door and switched off the harsh overhead lights.

My eyes filled with tears as I watched my son sit back down in the chair he had spent far too much time in over the past several days. His introduction to the world had been a harsh one—born two months premature as his birth mother lost her life to a heroin overdose, months spent in an incubator in the hospital NICU, two heart surgeries and countless drug treatments —but painful as those months were for both of us, our kangaroo care time had been a blessing in the midst of all that tragedy.

If I had never made all those wrong turns in my earlier years, I wouldn't have ended up at that N.A. meeting where I met Brandy. Maybe they hadn't been wrong turns after all. How could they be, if they'd brought me to this beautiful boy who had entered the world all alone? If my suffering was necessary to lead me to Danny—to make me worthy to adopt him—then every second of it was well worth it. I would endure it again a hundred times over to bring the two of us together.

Danny motioned to the overhead lights and whispered, "Is that better, Mom?"

"Yes," I whispered as my eyes filled with tears, "I love you, Danny. You gave my life purpose, you know."

A tear slid down Danny's cheek as he whispered, "I love you, Mom. I always felt kind of guilty that you spent so much time on us, and you never married."

I felt my childhood friend touch a hand to my shoulder.

You were right, Danny, **I told him without breaking eye contact with my son,** *I never did find a man to love as much as you.*

I could hear my friend's smile in the tone of his voice. Do you regret never getting married, Abbie?

I smiled at my son. *No, I don't. I lived a good life. If I had it to do all over again, I wouldn't change a single thing.*

Truth be told, I had gone on some dates in the years after Collin's death but—although I'd never admit it to anyone—I could never love any man.

My heart would always belong to the angel who had helped me get over the loss of Collin. Real or not, no man could ever measure up to my Castiel.

22

"And So It Goes"
Billy Joel

I t was two o'clock in the morning and I was sitting in the rocking chair that Judy had bought for me the day I adopted Danny. There was something magical about this quiet time in the middle of the night, when the old day was barely over, the new day had just begun and most of the world was still fast asleep. It was a magic that I'd never even realized existed until I became a mother. I looked down at the precious baby sleeping in my arms. He'd been home with me for three months now and I still had a hard time laying him down in his crib at night. My sweet boy had been through so much in his short life. I just didn't have the heart to put him down when he looked so content in my arms.

"And So It Goes" by Billy Joel was playing softly from the speaker across the room. I had to admit, the song made an achingly beautiful lullaby. A smile spread across my face as I pictured my childhood friend, listening to the same song as he watched over us from somewhere far away.

As I listened to the lyrics, my thoughts drifted to my angel and my eyes filled with tears. I hadn't worked up the courage to watch an episode of *Supernatural*, since the morning I'd woken up and realized that the best days of my life weren't real. But in that darkened room with my baby sleeping peacefully in my arms, I found myself longing to see my angel's face again.

I let out a defeated sigh as I leaned over the arm of the rocking chair and inched the remote on the end table closer to me with the tips of my fingers until I was able to pick it up. Then I shook my head at my own stupidity as I turned on the television and started up Netflix. As images of recommended shows and shows that I'd partially watched filled the screen, I held my breath. I was probably going to regret reopening this old wound, but I needed to see his face. So, I selected the search function, keyed in the letters for *Supernatural* and selected the show as soon as it popped up on the screen. Then I bit my lip and scrolled through the seasons, debating which episode might hurt the least to watch.

After a bit of hemming and hawing, I chose the third episode from season nine. "I'm no Angel" had always been one of my favorites. Whenever I watched it, I was moved by the humble acceptance in human Castiel's eyes as he dealt with his unfortunate circumstances without ever complaining or feeling sorry for himself. That sweet kindness in his eyes was the closest thing to my angel's infinitely compassionate eyes that I'd ever witnessed on the show.

I left Billy Joel's quiet lullaby playing on repeat as I started up the episode. I didn't need absolute silence to watch the show. I already knew every line by heart, and I was hoping the music might afford a certain measure of detachment that'd make it easier to watch the television angel with the face of the angel who'd stolen my heart. *Was that completely messed up?* Maybe, but no one else was around to witness my temporary lapse in good judgment.

There in the dark with my beautiful baby sleeping in my arms, I wept for my angel and his lonely existence. Real or not, I whispered the goodbye that he'd never given me the chance to utter and insane as it was, I prayed for God to watch over my angel—who probably didn't even exist—and help him find his way back home to heaven.

At some point during the episode, I drifted off to sleep. Billy Joel's song played softly in the background of my dream as Castiel sat on the couch, watching over me and Danny from the other side of the room. We didn't exchange any words in the dream. He just smiled at me with as much sorrow in his eyes as the fictional Castiel onscreen, who was listening to the woman ahead of him in church pray for God to send his angels to heal her sick husband. I wanted to get up and go to my guardian angel but my limbs were paralyzed, probably because some section of my mommy brain realized that my infant was still in my arms and it wasn't safe to move.

When I woke up, an episode of *Supernatural* several past the one I'd selected was playing. Stupid as it was, I turned my head toward the couch where Castiel had sat watching over us in my dream. He wasn't there, of course. No one was in the room but me and Danny, but I could handle that.

I wasn't alone in the world anymore. This beautiful boy in my arms was with me, and I had my dream angel to thank for leading me to him in a roundabout way...

...I could still hear Billy Joel's "And So It Goes" playing in the distance as I woke up in the hospital room. Cassie was back. She was sitting in a folding chair near her brother, and my dear childhood friend was crouching on the floor between the two of them. Both of my children sat with their heads bowed and their hands clasped in prayer as my friend whispered to them.

I knew they couldn't hear his words, but my eyes filled with tears as I listened to him.

Danny touched their clasped hands as he murmured, "It's time for you to let your mother go now."

Cassie let out a soft whimper, as if she had actually heard him.

My friend gave Cassie's clasped hands a squeeze as he whispered, "You need to let her know that you'll be okay after she's gone, Cassie." *Then he turned toward his namesake and whispered in his ear,* "Be strong for your sister, Danny. Tell your mother that you're going to take care of Cassie, and let her know that it's okay for her to let go."

A tear slid down my son's cheek, as if he had heard my friend too. In fact, I almost could have sworn I saw him nod in response to Danny's words.

My dear friend smiled as he touched Danny's head. "Your mother is in a lot of pain, but she won't leave until you both tell her that it's alright to let go."

Then my friend looked up at me and smiled, and I drifted back to the past...

...Danny was five years-old and the two of us were sitting on his bed, reading bedtime stories.

As I shut the first of our books for the night, he looked up at me with his beautiful big brown eyes. "At school today, Jake told me that he's going to be a big brother soon."

I smiled at him and tried to conceal the worry that had often kept me up at night. *Was Danny missing out on something, being with just me? Would he be better off with a sibling?* I'd been toying with the idea of adopting another child for a while. In fact, I had looked into foster care just a few weeks earlier. "Would you like to have a little brother or sister some-day, Danny?"

"I'm not sure," he muttered with the impeccable honesty of a kindergartener.

My smile widened as I replied, "You know, there are lots of kids out there who need good families to love them."

Danny scratched his head and scrunched up his face as he pondered that for a moment. Then he looked up at me with a smile that absolutely melted my heart. "Well, we're a good family."

I kissed the top of his head as I picked up the next book from the pile he'd selected. "Then maybe we should think about sharing our love with another little boy or girl."

"Maybe we should," Danny muttered with a yawn as he snuggled closer to me to help me hold the book and turn the pages...

As luck would have it, I received a call just three weeks later. A newborn baby girl had been abandoned in a bathroom at a public library not far from where we lived. The doctors said it was clear that her mother hadn't given much thought to proper prenatal care, and the infant had several medical issues as a result of that neglect. They contacted me because of my recent interest in foster care and all my experience with Danny's medical issues when he was a baby.

My beautiful baby girl came home to live with us nine weeks later, after an extended stay in the hospital NICU. I toyed with names for a while before settling on the only one that seemed to fit. My son was named after one of the two most important figures in my life, my dear childhood friend. It only seemed right that my daughter be named after the other one, the angel who held my heart. So, I named her Cassie, after my dear Castiel.

Danny was a wonderful big brother to Cassie right from the start. Of course, he lovingly teased his little sister for sport now and then as they grew older, but he never hesitated to swoop in and protect her from harm.

...It was a glorious early spring evening, one of the first after a brutal winter that'd seemed intent on sticking around forever. The air wafting in from the open window above the kitchen sink filled the room with the blissful aroma of freshly mowed grass. Danny and Cassie were playing in the backyard while I fixed dinner. I could just make out the gleeful sounds of their laughter over the distant hum of a neighbor's lawn mower.

I smiled to myself as I opened the cupboard, took out three plates and set them out on the table. This was a welcome change of pace from the nonstop bickering that had echoed through the stale air in our house at the tail end of winter. Squabbles between my two children had become such a constant that I was beginning to feel more like a referee than a mother. They would never seriously injure each other, but four-year-old Cassie certainly didn't hesitate to jump on her big brother to snatch a toy from his hand. Danny normally had the patience of a saint when it came to his little sister's antics, but cabin fever had frayed his nerves by winter's end and I'd caught him giving her a resentful shove on more than one occasion. In fact, that was part of the reason why the kitchen window was open. The breath of spring air drifting in through the screen was delightful, but it was my vigilant readiness to run out and referee that had prompted me to open the window.

I grabbed three napkins, folded them in half and put one beside each plate. Then I opened the silverware drawer and gathered three sets of utensils, but a blood curdling scream from the backyard made me drop them back in the drawer.

I raced out the backdoor, prepared to scold Danny for whatever offense had prompted his sister's cry but after bounding down three steps, I caught sight of Danny struggling to carry his sister toward the house. Like a cat struggling to break free from a toddler's unceremonious grasp, Cassie was gradually slipping lower in her brother's arms as she squirmed and bawled inconsolably.

I rushed down the remaining steps and met them at the base of the stairs. "What happened?"

"I don't know," Danny muttered as he handed his wriggling sister over to me. "She just started screaming and grabbing her foot, so I picked her up off the ground."

I carried Cassie into the house with Danny following close on my heels. Then I plopped into the nearest kitchen chair, holding Cassie on my lap. A scowl of brotherly concern furrowed Danny's young brow as he dropped into the chair beside us.

I tugged off my daughter's sandal. "Can you tell me what happened, Cas?"

"I think I stepped on a bee," she whimpered.

Danny hopped up from the table and raced out of the room as his sister broke down in tears all over again.

While I was inspecting Cassie's foot for the stinger, her big brother returned carrying his favorite stuffed dinosaur, the toy they'd been fighting over earlier that day. He held it out to her with an infectious grin. "Do you want to hold onto Rex, Cas? I think you need him more than me now."

Cassie's crying died off as she nodded and took the toy from her brother's hands.

The smile that spread across Danny's face as his sister hugged the dinosaur to her chest filled me with parental pride...

...It took some time to orient myself when I resurfaced in the present this time. Panic gripped me as I surveyed the dimly lit hospital room. Danny and Cassie were still sitting next to each other in those God-awful folding chairs at my bedside. My childhood friend was sitting on the bed beside me, holding my hand in his...but I was standing and watching them from a corner of the room near the windows.

My dear friend smiled at me as he stood up from the bed and crossed the room to join me in the corner. "It's alright, Abbie. I'm going to be right here with you till the end."

I dropped my head to Danny's shoulder as I watched my beautiful children pray for me. "Do we have to go now?"

Danny shook his head and whispered, "No, not until you're ready."

I silently thanked God that my friend was there with me at the end of everything as I turned to face him. "Then why can I see myself?"

My friend wrapped an arm around my shoulders and touched his head to mine. "Your pain is too intense now. It will be easier for you like this. We don't have to leave just yet, but it will be time soon."

I nodded as the two of us sat down on the floor in the corner. Then I dropped my head to Danny's shoulder and slipped back to the past...

...It was a Friday afternoon about three weeks into the new school year, and Cassie and I were baking chocolate chip cookies for our special night together. Danny was sleeping over at a friend's house. So, we were planning to enjoy a girls' night at home, painting our nails, eating junk food and staying up late to watch movies.

Cassie's first grade year seemed to have gotten off to a pretty rocky start. She had been moody and withdrawn since the school year began, and I was hoping our alone time might encourage her to open up about what was going on.

Cassie was scooping balls of cookie dough onto the baking sheets, and helping herself to the occasional spoonful when she thought I wasn't looking, while I was taking care of baking the cookies in the oven. She swallowed the bite of cookie dough she'd snuck as I turned from the oven to carry the latest batch of cookies to the counter to cool. "Mom," she muttered as she looked up at me with her beautiful big blue eyes, "Did you have lots of friends when you were my age?"

I smiled at her as I pulled out the chair beside hers and sat down at the table. "No, Cas. Actually, I just had one very dear friend."

"Danny," she whispered, "That was the boy you named Danny after, right?"

A wistful smile spread across my face at the mention of my dear childhood partner-in-crime. "Yes. It was, but it took me and Danny a while to find each other. Before we became friends, I felt pretty alone."

The hurt in Cassie's innocent young eyes tugged at my heartstrings as she whispered, "You did?"

"Yes." I tucked a wayward curl behind her ear to keep it from dropping into the bowl of cookie dough in front of her. "There were plenty of nights when I cried myself to sleep because the other kids at school weren't very kind to me."

Tears swam in her lovely blue eyes as she nodded. "Sometimes the kids in my new class aren't very kind to me either."

"I'm so sorry to hear that," I whispered as I leaned closer and planted a tender kiss on her forehead. "I know how much that hurts."

"Jada calls me a loser," she muttered as her eyes dropped to the bowl on the table in front of her, "She says I always know all the answers in school because I spend all my time reading because…I don't have any friends."

My heart thumped with maternal longing to pull her out of there and homeschool her to protect her from those monstrous little predators, but then I thought of my dear childhood friend. If my mother had pulled me out of school, I never would have met Danny. He would have been left to face the predators all on his own, and I would've gone on feeling lonely and unloved. Painful as the lesson was for both of us, I knew Cassie needed to learn how to deal with difficult situations and make friends to help her weather the inevitable storms life would bring her way.

My daughter looked up at me and whispered, "How did you meet your friend Danny?"

I grabbed a spoon from the table, scooped a bite of cookie dough from the bowl and winked at her as I placed it in her hand. She giggled, and I stroked a loving hand over her curls as she popped it in her mouth. "I used to sit all alone in the cafeteria at lunch," I confessed, "in the farthest corner from the mean girls who teased me. Then one day, Danny just walked up to my table. He asked if I'd like some company and when I nodded, he sat down across from me with a shy little half-smile on his face. I don't really remember what we talked about, but I remember how happy it made me feel to have somebody to sit with."

Cassie's brow furrowed as she swallowed the cookie dough in her mouth. "Maybe I should find somebody who's sitting alone and ask if they want company."

"That sounds like a great idea to me," I whispered, "Thank you for sharing what's going on in your life with me, Cas. I know that wasn't easy for you to talk about."

A conspiratorial grin spread across her sweet face as she picked up another spoon, scooped a bite of cookie dough from the bowl and handed it to me. "Thanks for making me feel a little bit better, Mommy. I'd be a lot sadder if I didn't have you and Danny to come home to."

Cassie found her own partner-in-crime soon after that conversation. The classroom predators had been picking on a sweet little girl named Maya during gym class because she had a lazy eye and wore thick glasses to correct her vision. My daughter used her ice cream money to buy Maya an ice cream sandwich, then asked if she could sit down and join her for lunch when she offered it to her. The two became inseparable after that. In fact, Maya spent so much time at our house over the years that Danny often joked he had two little sisters.

I always saw something of myself in sweet little Maya, the child who made life at school much more bearable for my daughter. From what I could gather, Maya's mother was a bit like mine, stingy with the gestures of affection and not very big on doling out praise. Like Danny, I was more than happy to count Maya as a member of our family. I liked to think that maybe our happy home made her life a little easier...

...My consciousness drifted back to the present, just enough to hear my son's voice close by my ear. "We're still here with you, Mom."

Before I could even think about trying to respond, the past swallowed me again...

...It was early in the evening on a school night. My fifteen-year-old son and I were sitting on the living room couch watching an episode of *Supernatural* together. It was one of my favorite times of the day. Now that Danny was a teenager, spending time with his mom wasn't exactly at the top of his priority list but a few months earlier, he'd walked in the room while I was watching an episode of my favorite show from my teenage years. It caught his attention enough to sit down and watch with me till the end of the episode. In fact, he enjoyed it so much that we started watching *Supernatural* together every evening, beginning with the first episode of season one the very next day.

Danny loved the show just as much as I always had, but tonight he seemed preoccupied. He kept glancing at his watch and looking over at me every few minutes. I noticed, but waited for him to bring up whatever was on his mind.

When the episode ended, I let the credits roll as I waited for Danny to decide whether he wanted to talk about what was troubling him.

He just sat there fidgeting for a few minutes with his eyes glued to the screen. Then he grabbed the remote from the coffee table and turned the television off with a resolute sigh as he shifted sideways on the couch to face me. "Mom?"

I turned toward him and smiled. "Yes?"

He pulled his legs up onto the couch and dropped his eyes to a frayed thread on the cuff of his jeans, twisting it in his fingers as he muttered, "Can we...talk for a minute?"

"Of course, Danny," I whispered with a nod, that he didn't see because his eyes were still fixed on that stray thread of denim. "I always have time to talk to you."

"There's something I…" His voice trailed off as he toyed with that thread, staring fixedly at it, as if it were the most interesting thing in the world. "There's something I want…to tell you."

Fairly certain that I knew where this conversation was headed, I reached across the empty couch cushion between us and gave his free hand an encouraging squeeze. "You can tell me anything, Danny. I'm always here for you."

His beautiful big brown eyes filled with tears as he looked up at me and squeezed my hand back.

"Talk to me," I whispered, unable to keep my own eyes from filling with tears. Nothing hurt me more than seeing one of my children in pain.

A tear slid down Danny's cheek as he bit his lip, hesitating as if he were afraid to break the silence.

"I love you," I whispered as I slid a little closer to him, "There is nothing you could ever tell me that would change that. I hope you know that."

More tears spilled down Danny's cheeks as he nodded and muttered, "I do."

"Good," I murmured as I gave his hand another squeeze. "Then take your time. I'm not going anywhere."

"Promise?" he muttered in an unsteady voice that cut through me like a knife.

"Cross my heart," I whispered as I wiped a tear from my cheek with my free hand, "Talk to me, Danny."

"I think…" My son dropped his eyes to our joined hands and took a deep breath, then muttered, "I'm like your friend Danny was…"

I smiled and gave his hand another squeeze as I waited for him to say it, because I knew he needed to say the words and see my reaction so there'd be no doubt in his mind.

"I um," he muttered as he looked up at me, "I like boys. I mean…I *like* them, like them."

I smiled at him and whispered, "I know, Danny."

I could see the tension visibly seep from his body as he muttered, "You do?"

"I've known for years," I whispered with a nod, "I love you with all my heart, Danny. All I've ever wanted is for you to be happy and true to yourself. I am proud of you. I will always be proud of you, and I will always be here for you."

Danny let out a sob as he slid closer and wrapped his arms around me, and I hugged him back like both our lives depended on it...

...Looking back on it all these years later, I had to wonder. Was it just coincidence that my son was gay, just like my dear childhood friend? It'd always broken my heart, how much my friend had feared his parents' reaction. He never came out to anyone but me because he was so terrified that his parents wouldn't accept him, if they knew who he truly was. Maybe that was one of the reasons why fate had brought my son into my life.

There wasn't much time to ponder that before the next memory came...

...It was well past Cassie's bedtime, but I was pretty sure she was still wide awake. She'd come out of school after the eighth-grade dance, red-eyed and sniffing back tears, but she'd made it perfectly clear when she hopped in the car that she was in no mood to talk about it. Sadly, she was nearing the age when kids tend to share less and less with their parents. Still, I wasn't about to stop trying.

I tapped my knuckles on her bedroom door and waited for her to welcome me in. When she mumbled a faint invitation from the other side of the door, I opened it. The only illumination in her pitch-dark room was the sliver of light that spilled in from the hall as I stepped inside. She pushed herself up to a seated position as I crossed the room and sat down on the edge of her bed. For some silly reason, I couldn't help thinking of the angel I'd often imagined perched on the edge of my bed during the lonely nights of my adolescence. "Do you want to talk about it?"

"Nobody asked me to dance," she muttered as her eyes dropped to her pillow. "All the other girls got asked."

"I never got asked to dance in junior high or high school," I admitted with a sympathetic smile.

"Oh great," she grunted, "So, I'm going to be a loser for four more years?"

"That was a hurtful thing to say," I whispered, although I didn't take it personally. She was just lashing out because she was in pain. Still, it was my job to remind her that wasn't okay.

"Sorry," she muttered under her breath as she looked up at me, "I just..."

"You're disappointed," I whispered, "I get it, and I wish I could tell you that it happened sooner for me."

There was a moment of silence before she muttered, "When *did* it happen?"

"I met plenty of nice boys when I went off to college," I replied with a grin, "but I didn't really feel butterflies in my stomach until the night my college boyfriend first caught my eye across a crowded room."

Despite her glum mood, Cas smiled at that. "What was his name?"

I hesitated a second, almost wishing I hadn't brought Collin up. I had never mentioned him to either of my children before. "His name was Collin."

She shifted sideways to look me in the eye. "How long did you date him?"

I swallowed back the sob that was inching its way up my throat. "Three years."

My daughter's eyes widened with curiosity as she muttered, "So, why didn't it last?"

"Because he passed away," I replied in a hoarse whisper. *She wasn't old enough to hear the rest of the details.*

My daughter's eyes welled with tears as she asked, "And you never met anybody else?"

"No..." A lump formed in my throat as that delusional night I'd spent dancing in Castiel's arms sprang to mind. *No one I got to keep.* "There was never anyone else like Collin." *And no one could ever measure up to my angel.* "But I don't have any regrets because I was blessed with you and Danny."

Cas dropped her eyes to her pillow again. "What if I never find anybody?"

"You will," I assured her. "Your somebody is out there right now, wondering when he'll be lucky enough to find you."

A sorrowful chuckle hiccupped from her mouth. "I'm not so sure about that."

"Well, I am," I murmured. I didn't doubt it for a second. She was too kind-hearted and lovable to end up alone...

...Again, I heard faint voices in the present. Danny and Cassie were carrying on a whispered conversation, but I couldn't stay in the present long enough to grasp their words. The last thought to cross my mind as I drifted back to the past, was how thankful I was that they had each other to lean on...

...I was reading in my bedroom when I heard Danny come in the front door. Now that my nineteen-year-old son was home for the summer after his first year of college, I tried to respect his privacy. After all, he was a young adult who came and went as he pleased when he was away at school. Still, I had a hard time falling asleep until I knew that he was home safe.

I stayed in my room, listening to the comforting echo of his footsteps as he advanced down the hall. Rushing out to greet him would only make it obvious that I'd been waiting up. Even if I hadn't normally felt the need to stay up until Danny got home, I doubt I could've fallen asleep that night while I knew Cassie was still upset about the dance.

Once I heard Danny shut his door, I slipped out of bed and tiptoed out into the hall. An irrational flicker of concern flitted through my mind when I realized my son's bedroom door was still open, his light was off and his room was empty.

Then I heard Danny's voice, somewhat muffled behind the closed door to Cassie's room. "Boys are stupid at your age."

"Plenty of other girls got asked to dance," Cassie muttered.

"Sure," Danny replied without missing a beat, "The cocky guys will ask the flirty girls to dance in eighth grade but trust me, those aren't the boys you want to notice you. The sweet guys who'll treat you like gold are still too shy to talk to girls at your age."

"Whatever," Cassie muttered.

"It's true," Danny assured her, "The best guys need more time to come out of their shells."

"How do you know what the best guys in my class need?"

"Because I'm one of the good guys," I could hear Danny's smile in the tone of his voice as he added, "and I was just starting to toy with the idea of coming out of my shell at your age."

"Well…" There was a short pause as Cassie considered her brother's response. "When did you get brave enough to talk to somebody you liked?"

"A few years later."

"So, what happened when you talked to him?"

"Not much," Danny admitted matter-of-factly, "because he was one of the good ones too. He was still too shy to dance, even when somebody else was brave enough to do the asking."

"Great," Cassie muttered, "So I'm cursed to be alone for years. Why does everybody in this family take forever to find somebody who likes them?"

"Ouch," Danny chuckled, "*I* like you now."

"Yeah," Cassie grumbled, although there was a hint of amusement in her sullen tone, "that's not the kind of *like* I'm talking about, and you know it!"

"Whatever, squirt," he murmured, "Trust me. It'll happen soon enough. Until then, you've got *somebody* who loves you a whole lot. I know I'm just your big brother, but I've always got time for you and I'm a pretty damn good listener."

"Yeah, you are." After a pause she asked, "When do boys stop being stupid?"

"I'll let you know when I get there," he teased.

I couldn't stop myself from grinning at the sound of my daughter's laughter.

"I've got a stash of chocolate hidden in my room," Danny confessed in a loud whisper, "What do you say we stay up past your bedtime and watch a movie together?"

"Can we watch *The Lucky One*?"

"I don't know that one," Danny muttered, "What's it about, and who's in it?"

"It's a love story," Cassie replied, giggling at her brother's groan of protest. "It's got Zac Efron and—"

"Stop right there," Danny interrupted, "You had me at Zac Efron. I'll go grab the junk food."

A smile spread across my face as I headed back down the hall to my room…

…For a moment, the past and present merged as my daughter's quiet laughter drew me toward the present day, but the past pulled me back before I could even get my bearings there…

…Cassie was positively beaming as she stepped into the crowded dining area of the restaurant. She waved and grinned at the two of us as she crossed the room and headed toward our table.

When she reached us, her brother and I stood up from our chairs and took turns hugging her. It filled my heart with so much joy to have the three of us together in the same room for the first time in months. Since Cassie and her husband had moved down south, these lunches of ours were few and far between, which made me treasure each one all the more. I couldn't complain. Both of my children were happy. *Life was good.*

"Okay, spill," Danny muttered as he pulled his younger sister's chair out from the table for her.

She answered him with a giddy chuckle as she scooted her chair closer to the table.

"I'm with Danny," I whispered as I sat back down, "Why are you glowing like that?"

Cassie's eyes filled with tears as an ear-to-ear grin spread across her face. "Matt and I are going to have a baby."

My own eyes filled with tears as I jumped up from my seat to hug my daughter. "I am so happy for you, Cas."

"You're going to be an amazing grandma," she whispered in my ear as she hugged me back…

…The memories were coming and going faster now, offering just fleeting glimpses of the major moments, as if the director of my montage was getting anxious to

wrap things up. I didn't have long to linger on that thought before the next memory replaced the last...

...Danny smiled at his husband and squeezed his hand as the elevator doors closed, shutting the three of us off from the rest of the world.

I pushed the button for the third floor as they exchanged a tender glance, and I couldn't help grinning to myself. Keith had made my son so happy. Both of my children had been blessed with such loving spouses. What more could a mother possibly ask for?

The bouquet of pink and white balloons in Keith's free hand bounced gleefully in the air as he leaned over and planted a kiss on my son's cheek. Danny's free arm was wrapped around a massive white teddy bear with a pink bow around its neck, and I was holding a lovely assortment of pink and white flowers in a crystal vase with a pink ribbon.

As the elevator doors opened onto the maternity floor, a rosy-cheeked doctor with snow white hair and a well-trimmed beard grinned at the three of us. "First baby in the family?"

I felt my cheeks blush to match the color of our gifts as I met his knowing eyes and chuckled. "How could you tell?"

"Just a hunch," he whispered as he winked at me and stepped onto the elevator.

Cassie's room was just a few feet away from the elevator. I knocked softly on the door, hoping we wouldn't wake her if she was sleeping.

Matt opened the door a few seconds later with a bleary-eyed smile. As I hugged him, he whispered, "Come on in and meet your granddaughter."

"I thought you'd never ask," I murmured, stepping farther into the room while Danny and Keith shook Matt's hand.

Cassie greeted me with a beaming smile, then dropped her eyes to the tiny infant sleeping in her arms.

My eyes filled with tears as I approached her bedside and got my first look at my granddaughter's face. She was absolutely perfect.

"Would you like to hold her?" Cassie whispered.

I nodded and carefully took the beautiful baby girl from my daughter. As I held my newborn grandchild in my arms, I glanced down at her cherubic face, then looked up at the smiling faces of my loved ones, all gathered together to celebrate this new addition to our family. Silly as it sounds, I couldn't help wishing that I could go back in time and show my younger self how much joy awaited me in the future...

...The instant that memory faded, the next took its place...

...I was tucked in a sunny corner of my cozy one-story retirement home in the suburbs, curled up in my favorite armchair with a blanket over my legs and a book in my hands. Danny's music was playing softly in the background, and I was finding it difficult to focus on the story I was trying to read. As Billy Joel's "And So It Goes" began to play, I gave up trying and sat the book face down on my lap. Then I dropped my head against the back of the chair and let the music carry me away.

In quiet moments like this when no one else was around, I almost swore I could feel a faint echo of my guardian angel's comforting touch. I shook my head at my own foolishness but silly as it was to hold onto such childish notions, the thought actually brought me a great deal of comfort in my golden years. The idea that an angel was watching over me as my body inched closer to death was incredibly appealing.

"Thanks for everything," I whispered to the empty room.

I grinned to myself as I imagined a whispered echo of my Castiel's touch brushing across my wrinkled cheek.

From out of nowhere, an ache flared in my chest, robbing the breath from my lungs. I squeezed my eyes shut as my body instinctively tensed against the pain.

I opened my eyes as the ache subsided. The room around me had gone all fuzzy, as if God had taken out his cosmic eraser and smudged my little corner of the world into nothing more than a blur of muted colors. But it didn't frighten me, because this was nothing new. These episodes were becoming more and more frequent with each passing day.

My health was failing. I'd known it for a while now, and I had made my peace with it. I'd lived a good long life, and I was ready for God to take me…

…*When I resurfaced in the present, my friend and I were sitting cross-legged on the floor in the corner of my hospital room, side by side with our heads touching.*

I smiled and turned my head to look him in the eyes. "You know, I haven't been able to sit like this in decades."

Danny answered with a carefree chuckle that made his eyes sparkle like they used to all those years ago, when it was just the two of us and he was truly happy because he didn't have to pretend to be anything he wasn't. "That was just your shell," *he whispered as he nodded toward my feeble torso on the bed across the room.*

I glanced down, and my eyes widened as I raised my arms and gawked at the youthful pair of hands attached to them.

"We love you, Mom," my son whispered from the other side of the room.

My eyes filled with tears as I looked toward the hospital bed and watched my son and daughter exchange teary-eyed smiles. They were seated on either side of my frail little body now, each of them holding onto one of my wrinkled hands.

"You've done your job, Mom," Cassie muttered as tears streamed down her cheeks, "You did such a wonderful job and we feel so blessed to be your children...but we know that you're hurting now...and we want you to know, Danny and I are going to be okay."

I stood up from the floor and stepped toward the bed as I listened to my children's words.

"It's okay to let go now, Mom," my son whispered. "I promise you, I'm going to look after Cassie. You won't be leaving us alone. We've got each other to lean on...and we have our husbands...we're both going to be just fine."

Keith was standing behind Danny's chair with a hand resting on his shoulder for support. Cassie's husband wasn't in the room. I figured he must be at home with the baby, but I was pretty sure I'd heard

Matt's voice whispering to Cassie earlier while I was fading in and out. I honestly could not have hand-picked better spouses for my children if I'd tried to. My son and daughter were both loved, and they would have each other to lean on...after I was gone.

My friend Danny stepped up beside me and wrapped an arm around my shoulders. "You're too far gone to speak to them now but if you concentrate, you can squeeze their hands to let them know you can hear them."

I was just about to ask Danny how to do that when I saw my wrinkled hands twitch in my children's.

They smiled at each other across my bed, and I knew that they would be alright after I left them.

I wanted so badly to tell them how much I loved them, and how happy they had both made me.

Danny tightened his supportive half-hug around my shoulders. "They know, Abbie."

I nodded and concentrated on squeezing my children's hands.

23

"Can't Help Falling In Love"

Kina Grannis

---

*T*he sky outside the window of my hospital room gradually darkened as my children sat on either side of my bed, reminiscing about our lives together, thanking me for everything I had done for them, assuring me that it was okay to let go when I was ready.

The two of them would be alright after I passed on. I knew that they would and yet, the thought of leaving them forever kept my spiritual body's feet cemented to the floor of that room.

My childhood friend stood beside me, holding onto my hand for support without putting any pressure on me to leave. I knew that I couldn't stay for much longer. Still, I appreciated Danny's patience during these final hours with my children.

Tears streamed down my cheeks as I turned away from my deathbed and walked to the window to gaze up at the star-speckled sky. It was such a beautiful clear night. There wasn't a single cloud in the sky to obstruct my view of the stars. Somehow I knew that I would never see the sun rise again, but I was alright with that. It seemed fitting that my final hours with my children should be these magical hours in the middle of the night, with them whispering their hushed goodbyes to me while the rest of the world was sound asleep. When they were infants, I'd spent so many of these peaceful nighttime hours in my rocking chair with them nestled safely in my arms as I lulled them off to dreamland. Now they were lulling me off to whatever came after this.

For some foolish reason, my thoughts drifted to that night long ago when I fell asleep in the rocking chair with Danny in my arms, while I was watching Supernatural for the first time in ages. I smiled to myself as I shook my head. Even now, mere hours away from my death, I just couldn't let go of that delusional three-day period of my life that I'd spent with my imaginary angel.

Behind me, my children continued to whisper soothing words to me—reminding me of memories we shared, promising me that they'd be okay, that it was alright for me to let go now. As I listened to their sweet voices, the melody that I'd heard playing in the distance during my much earlier lucid hours in the hospital began to play again.

I grinned, remembering the way that my son had so readily accepted it as something from the great beyond that only I could hear, and how much that had irritated his sister. Cassie hadn't been ready to let me go then but she seemed to have made her peace with it now, thanks to some subliminal coaxing from my childhood friend.

So, why was I still here?

Something was holding me back. I just couldn't pinpoint what that something was. It was almost like having a word on the tip of my tongue that I could practically taste, but I couldn't quite vocalize for some inexplicable reason.

The melody playing in the distance was so soft and sweet, familiar but not entirely so.

I lifted my hand to touch the window pane as I admired the last night sky that I would ever set eyes on, but my hand couldn't quite connect with the glass.

This world was fading, or I suppose it was me that was fading away.

It seemed as though I ought to be terrified and heartbroken at the thought of deserting my children for the rest of their days, but that song playing in the distance was making it impossible for me to feel sorrow or fear. I felt entirely at peace as the music gradually *grew louder, until I was finally able to decipher the lyrics.*

This wasn't the Elvis Presley version of the song. The singer of this soft sweet version was a female with an airy ethereal voice. Still, as soon as I heard the words to "Can't Help Falling In Love," I marveled at the fact that I hadn't recognized the tune right away, considering the memory it was anchored to.

"You weren't ready to accept it yet," a voice behind me murmured, in response to my unspoken thought.

The voice didn't belong to my childhood friend, or to either of my children.

Tears filled my eyes as I stared at the night sky beyond the window pane, too afraid to turn around or speak. This was obviously nothing more than a parting delusion—a painless way for my mind to transition from life to death as my body failed me—or perhaps my son had turned on the television, hoping my favorite show might offer me some comfort.

Castiel's voice had been the voice of comfort for me for so many years, but now—at the end of everything— that beautiful deep voice of his stung like a knife to the heart.

I heard someone step up behind me as the voice asked, "May I have this dance?"

Well, it definitely wasn't the television. That meant that one last senile delusion was the only plausible explanation. How fitting that my final moments should find me lapsing back into the madness of my youth.

I bit my lip as I stared at the window pane, wanting with all my failing heart to see my angel's reflection in the glass. But I didn't see anything.

"I suppose perhaps I deserve your silence," he murmured close behind me, "I am so sorry that I didn't say goodbye to you before I left that night, Abigail. I knew that if I did…" My delusion paused to clear his throat, then whispered, "I was afraid that if I stayed to say goodbye, you would convince me not to leave."

"Would that have been so terrible?" I muttered in a trembling voice, still afraid to turn around and look at him. This couldn't possibly be real.

"No, it would not have been terrible. It would have been magical," my imaginary angel replied in a gruff whisper, "but we would have burned in hell for it."

I opened my mouth to answer him, but I had no idea what to say to that.

"I might have considered choosing that path for myself," he whispered close to my ear, "but I could not allow that to happen to you, Abigail. Guiding you down the right path was my one true purpose here on earth. I could never allow myself to fail you."

I spun around, and a breathless sob escaped my throat as I came face to face with my angel. "You're really here?"

"I have always been here," he whispered as his own eyes filled with tears.

I nodded, then glanced around the room to ground myself because I felt as if I might float away. "Am I dreaming all of this?"

"No," he replied as he stood motionless, watching me inch closer to him, *"It is no longer necessary for us to meet in dreams."*

"Was it..." My voice faltered as his brilliant blue eyes locked with mine. They were even more beautiful than I remembered. *"Was it all just a dream? Those three days..."*

The sorrow in his eyes twisted the knife in my heart as he shook his head and whispered, "They were real."

"Then..." I dropped my gaze to that signature lopsided knot in his necktie and let the tears spill down my cheeks as I sobbed, *"Why didn't you leave anything behind...to let me know that it was real...that...I wasn't crazy?"*

He tipped his head forward and touched his forehead to mine, enveloping me in that all-encompassing sense of warmth and peace that I'd been so desperate to feel for so many years. "I thought it would be easier for you to let go and move on, if you believed it had all been a dream."

"I never moved on," I whispered as I lifted my eyes back to his.

He nodded and just that slight brush of flesh against flesh, as his forehead moved against mine, made me feel as if we were soaring above the clouds. "I know."

I reached up and concentrated on steadying my hand as I touched his cheek, still afraid that none of this was real. "Then...why did you stop visiting my dreams?"

He pulled his head back to get a better look at me, breaking that blissful point of contact between us. "I visited your dreams every night, Abigail."

"No, I never saw you again..." I muttered as my hand dropped from his cheek, "except for that one time when Danny was a baby..."

"That was the one time you chose to remember," Castiel replied with a heartrending smile, "The rest, you forgot because it was too painful for you to recall."

"But you had to remember all of it," I muttered in a rough whisper.

"Yes," he agreed as his eyes searched mine, "I did."

A tear slid down my cheek as I shook my head. "I'm so sorry."

"You have nothing to be sorry for, Abigail." He raised a tentative hand to my face as if he intended to touch my cheek, but lowered it with a broken exhalation as he murmured, "Just know that I was there by your

side every step of the way. I never truly left you, not for a second."

I threw my arms around his neck and buried my face against his shoulder as his arms wrapped around me, and I felt that cosmic shift just like I'd felt when we danced all those years ago. I lifted my head from his shoulder and smiled at him. "Is that dance invitation still on the table?"

Tears shimmered in his angelic eyes as he murmured, "Always."

He took my hand in his as he placed his other hand on my hip, and the music swelled as he led me around the room. His movements were so graceful and perfectly attuned to the melody that it felt a bit more like floating than dancing. I was vaguely aware of the world around us, and I knew I should still be worried about leaving before I got a chance to say my final goodbyes to my children, but all of my concerns began to fade as the music filled my ears.

A hushed exhalation across the room reminded me that my childhood friend was still behind us. I stopped moving, and so did my angel. Together, we turned and looked at Danny.

He was sitting on my hospital bed beside my failing body again. A smile spread across his face as he met my eyes. "Don't worry about me, Abbie. We've got all the time in the world to catch up. I've been taking up all *your time for a while now. I think it's only fair that I give your angel a turn."*

I nodded and looked up at Castiel with an apologetic frown. "I don't even know your real name."

"That is unimportant," he murmured with a knowing smile.

A lump formed in my throat as I whispered, "How could your name be unimportant?"

"I was a different angel when I was given that name," he replied as he touched my cheek with a wistful smile, "It was the name of a Watcher angel with a fixed set of orders that were set in stone and a moral compass that failed to point me in the right direction once those orders no longer came. You gave my existence a true purpose, Abigail. So, if it's all the same to you, I would prefer to keep the name that I took for you."

"I…" His hand on my cheek was filling me with so much warmth that it was difficult to focus on what I was trying to say. "I don't even know what you really look like."

He took my hand in his again and resumed the dance as he whispered, "Does it matter?"

I glanced over my shoulder at my own brittle body on that hospital bed across the room as I shook my head and whispered, "No."

"I see you, Abigail," my angel whispered, *"Not the physical husk that you are about to shed, but the soul within. I have always seen you."*

A tear slid down my cheek as I nodded, unable to come up with any words that were grand enough to express the way that he made me feel.

"And if you give it some thought," he whispered as *he whirled me around the room, "I think you'll realize that you have always seen me too."*

"So, what happens now?" I asked in a feeble whisper.

"Now, you finish your journey," he murmured close to my ear.

"No," I muttered as I leaned back to look him in the eyes, *"I mean, what happens to you now?"*

The ancient sorrow that had lurked in the recesses of his angelic eyes since the night I first met him dissipated in a radiant burst of light as he smiled at me. "Here you stand at the threshold of heaven, and you are concerned with what will become of me?"

"I care about you," I muttered around the massive lump in my throat. If I lost him again after this... I wanted no part of a heaven that didn't include my angel.

"I am so proud of you, Abigail," he whispered, *"You lived your life with such purpose. I told you to look for every opportunity to make a small difference in the lives*

of others. Instead, you made all the difference in the world to those two souls who are seated at your bedside."

"I took your message to heart," I whispered as I glanced back at my children, "and I followed your example."

His dance steps faltered as he tilted his head to one side and studied me through narrowed eyes. "How so?"

"I just did what you did," I muttered with a shrug.

He raised an eyebrow, wordlessly prompting me to explain what I meant by that.

"The moment I set eyes on Danny, I knew I had found my purpose," I whispered as I looked at my beautiful son, sitting at my bedside with my wrinkled hand clasped in his. "You said that, although it was impossible to be something to everyone, it was possible to be everything to someone. So, I devoted my life to being everything to my children, just like you discovered your true purpose when you realized that you were everything to me."

My beautiful angel grinned from ear to ear as he fell back into step with the music and whirled me around the room. "You misunderstood me."

I couldn't stop my eyes from welling with tears as I muttered, "What?"

"You did teach me a valuable lesson, Abigail, that being everything to someone is far more important than empty attempts to be something to everyone," he

whispered as he hugged me closer. "But perhaps I should have been clearer in my explanation."

I bit my lip as I fought to keep myself from breaking down in tears. "I don't understand."

"I realize that now," he murmured as he continued to sweep me along in time with the music, "When I said that you taught me that being everything to a single someone is of the greatest importance, I was not implying that I was your everything."

"Then what did you mean?" I muttered in a barely audible whisper.

"I meant that you are everything to me," he whispered, "You have been since the day I first met you."

I nodded, searching for my voice for a few breathless seconds before answering in a trembling whisper, "So...what happens now?"

As we stopped dancing, he released me from his arms. Then he held a hand out to me with a radiant smile. "Now, you say your goodbyes to those beautiful children that you devoted your life to."

I took his hand, unable to look away from him as we moved toward the bed.

My dear friend smiled at me from his spot beside my aged body as Castiel and I approached my bedside.

I nodded to him and forced a smile as my eyes drifted to my daughter, sitting in the chair beside him. A strangled sob escaped my throat as I walked up to my sweet baby girl and kissed the top of her head. It was an odd sensation, since I couldn't physically connect with her any longer. I looked up at Castiel and my breath caught in my throat before I could voice the question on the tip of my tongue.

"She can feel it," my angel whispered before I could work up the nerve to ask, "Just as you felt my touch in that church on the day of Danny's funeral."

"How?" I muttered as I glanced at my friend and marveled at how surreal it felt to be talking about his funeral when he was right there in front of us.

"You are not touching her shell," Castiel explained in a reverent tone, "You are touching her soul."

Tears spilled down my cheeks as I nodded, then bent to kiss my daughter's head again. "I love you, Cassie," I sobbed in a broken whisper, "with all my heart."

My shriveled hand squeezed my daughter's as I spoke to her soul, and she let out a muffled whimper as she squeezed mine back.

Then I walked around to the other side of the bed, where my son sat holding my other hand. I squeezed my eyes shut as I kissed his head and whispered, "I love you with all my heart, Danny. Thank you for giving my life purpose."

Tears slid down my son's cheeks as my aged hand squeezed his, and he smiled at his sister on the opposite side of the bed as he gently squeezed mine back.

It seemed as though I ought to feel grief in this moment, but I only felt peace and warmth as my angel held onto my new youthful hand. "What now?" I muttered as I looked up at him.

Castiel bent and kissed the top of my head. "Now, I take you home."

"Home," I echoed, exhaling the word like a sigh of relief, "Whose home? Yours...or mine?"

He wrapped his arms around me, and I felt every last trace of pain and worry—every old heartache, every internal scar—slip away in the warmth of his embrace as he replied, "Ours."

My dear childhood friend kissed my failing body's wrinkled cheek and bent to touch his forehead to hers, lingering there for a moment as he shut his eyes and whispered something too soft for me to hear. As Castiel released me from our embrace, my friend stood from the bed and took one of my youthful hands in his while my angel took the other. "I told you I'd be here with you till the end," my friend whispered with an affectionate grin.

Too emotional to speak, I nodded as the far side of my hospital room grew blindingly bright.

As the three of us stepped toward that light, I turned my head and looked over my shoulder at my beautiful children one last time.

"You'll come back to ease their passage when it is their time to move on," Castiel whispered beside my ear.

The last bit of heartache inside me crumbled away as I smiled at my children and whispered, "This isn't goodbye forever. It's just goodbye for now."

With that, I turned back to look at the light across the room. With each step the three of us took toward it, it grew brighter while the room around us faded.

As we stepped closer, that light bathed me in a warmth that filled me with far more joy and tranquility than sunlight ever had. "I thought I would never see sunlight again," I murmured as we moved closer.

Castiel smiled at me as we reached the threshold of our eternal home. "It's the darkness that you're leaving behind, Abigail. There will be nothing but light for you from now on and thanks to you, I can say the same for myself."

In loving memory of Joseph B. Monahan, Sr.

The depth of emotion that I experienced during your final days bleeds through the pages of this book. I will carry your final breath with me until we meet again.

A special thanks to Katie, Tara, Marsha, Kevin and Kristin for beta reading this story. You helped me make it so much stronger in the end.

Last but certainly not least, thank you to my editor, Kate Kenyon.

ERIN A. JENSEN

If you enjoyed reading this story, please consider leaving a review, giving it a shout out on social media, and/or telling your friends about it. Every penny earned by this book's sales will be donated to Random Acts charitable organization.

If you'd like to learn more about me, check out my website — erinajensen.com

You can also find me on Twitter— @ErinAJensen,

Facebook, and Goodreads.com

I enjoy connecting with readers to hear what you think about my stories; answer questions; or chat about books, *Supernatural*, or anything else we both happen to love!

37186732R00175

Made in the USA
Middletown, DE
23 February 2019